It couldn't b

You're an idiot. I

The voices were approaching. He could hear it again, the voice that sounded like hers, and he opened his eyes and watched as the small group spilled through the double doors and came onto the ward.

It *was* her.

Thinner, lines of strain around her eyes, her mid-brown hair longer, but unmistakably Annie. She was wearing theatre blues, baggy, soft cotton pyjamas that should have done nothing for her, but she looked stunning. He closed his eyes again just briefly, and when he opened them she was looking at him.

Her jaw dropped a fraction, then firmed, her shoulders straightening as if to resist a blow, and he felt a surge of regret for all the things that had happened to disturb the status quo. No, not for the things that had happened, but their effect at least.

'Annie,' he murmured, and he felt his mouth kick up in a crooked smile.

'Max.'

Caroline Anderson has the mind of a butterfly. She's been a nurse, a secretary, a teacher, run her own soft-furnishing business and now she's settled on writing. She says, 'I was looking for that elusive something. I finally realised it was variety, and now I have it in abundance. Every book brings new horizons and new friends, and in between books I have learned to be a juggler. My teacher husband John and I have two beautiful and talented daughters, Sarah and Hannah, umpteen pets and several acres of Suffolk that nature tries to reclaim every time we turn our backs!' Caroline also writes for the Mills & Boon Tender Romance® series.

Recent titles by the same author:

A VERY SINGLE WOMAN
THE PERFECT CHRISTMAS
ACCIDENTAL RENDEZVOUS
RESCUING DR RYAN
A MOTHER BY NATURE

ACCIDENTAL SEDUCTION

BY

CAROLINE ANDERSON

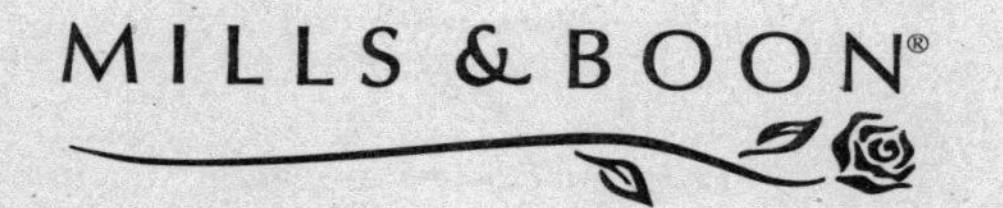

First published in Great Britain 2002
Harlequin Mills & Boon Limited,
Eton House, 18-24 Paradise Road, Richmond, Surrey TW9 1SR

ISBN 0 263 83082 9

Set in Times Roman 10½ on 12½ pt.
03-0802-44705

Printed and bound in Spain
by Litografia Rosés, S.A., Barcelona

CHAPTER ONE

MAX walked onto the ward and looked around, checking out the unfamiliar layout, the strange faces, the different uniforms. He felt a twinge of apprehension and dismissed it. He knew himself better than that. A couple of days and he'd be part of the team—except that this time he was the head of the team, the consultant, the one they'd all look to.

That ought to scare him, he thought, but it didn't. He was ready for it, champing at the bit. It was what he'd worked so hard for, for so many years—and it started now. With an inward girding of the loins he drew himself up, squared his shoulders and continued walking onto the ward.

'Can I help you?'

He turned his head and smiled at the nurse. 'Morning. I'm Max Williamson, the new—'

'Oh, Mr Williamson, we were expecting you—but probably a bit later. I'm Suzie Crane, one of the staff nurses. Come with me, I'll take you to meet Damien, the charge nurse.'

He followed her down the ward and into a treatment room, where a male nurse was just finishing taping up a dressing.

'Right, Ted, you'll do,' he said, and turned towards the newcomers. 'Hello, Suzie.' He scanned Max with curious eyes and stripped off his gloves, holding out a hand in greeting. 'Damien Rayner—and you must be Mr Williamson.'

'Max, please. It's good to meet you.'

'And you. You're good and early. Trying to create a good impression?'

Max chuckled. 'Just finding my feet. Someone's kindly scheduled my time so I don't really start till this afternoon, but I wanted to familiarise myself and meet everybody, and I thought this was the obvious place to start.'

'Quite so. Let's take five and grab a coffee. Ted, I'm going to leave you with Suzie, OK?'

'Perfectly all right.' The elderly man chuckled. 'She's a lot prettier than you.'

'You old flirt,' Suzie teased, and flicked the brakes off the bed. 'Come on, let's wheel you back before you get ideas.'

Max and Damien left them to it and headed back up the ward. As they walked Damien explained the layout, a very common and sensible system of bays and treatment areas, with small side rooms of one or two for critical patients right under the eye of the staff. A long desk bristling with computers and phones and monitoring equipment, the nursing station was set right in the centre of the ward and was the hub around which all the activity revolved.

Behind it was the ward office and a little kitchen, and Damien was just heading for the door when the phone rang and he was summoned.

'Typical. Give me a minute,' he said, and went into his office.

Max stood there for a moment looking round, and

then his ear caught a sound, a laughing voice that stopped him in his tracks.

It couldn't be.

He went still, his head raised slightly, listening for the sound again in the hubbub of the ward, but his heart had slammed against his ribs then settled to a steady roar, drowning out not only the voice but also reason and common sense.

You're an idiot. It can't be her, he told himself—and anyway, she's married.

It didn't stop you last time, his alter ego reminded him ruthlessly.

His heart still wasn't listening either. It was thrashing away inside his chest, threatening to choke him. He dragged in a much-needed lungful of air, propped himself casually against the wall and closed his eyes for a fraction of a second, praying for enough control that he didn't make a complete idiot of himself.

The voices were approaching. He could hear it again, the voice that sounded like hers, and he opened his eyes and watched as the small group spilled through the double doors and came onto the ward.

It *was* her.

Thinner, lines of strain around her eyes, her mid-brown hair longer now, scraped up in a ponytail, but unmistakably Annie. She was wearing theatre blues, baggy, soft cotton pyjamas that should have done nothing for her, but she looked stunning. He closed his eyes again just briefly, and when he opened them she was looking at him.

Her jaw dropped a fraction, then firmed, her shoulders straightening as if to resist a blow, and he felt a surge of regret for all the things that had happened to disturb the status quo. No, not for the things that had happened, but their effect, at least.

He shrugged away from the wall, hoping that she couldn't hear his heart thundering against his ribs.

'Annie,' he murmured, and he felt his mouth kick up in a crooked smile.

'Max.'

She made it sound like a prayer—only instead of a prayer of thanks, it sounded like a prayer for deliverance.

A voice interrupted them. 'Do you two know each other?'

Max turned his head to look at the man. Another surgeon, also in scrubs, his eyes searching. He recognised him from his interview. David somebody. Armstrong?

'We've met,' she said carefully, and Max nearly laughed.

Met? They'd done a damn sight more than meet—and yet they hadn't, really. He didn't know her surname, where she'd been for the past year and a bit, anything about her other than the simple fact that his body and his heart had recognised her the very first moment they'd first set eyes on each other at that hotel.

He held out his hand, and slowly, reluctantly almost, she placed her cool, firm palm against his and heat rocketed through him. His fingers curled around the back of her hand, seeking to prolong the brief contact, but she pulled it back, tucking it into her pocket as her eyes slid away.

'So what brings you here?' she asked with false brightness.

'My job. I've just started—I'm the new consultant general surgeon.'

Her eyes flew up to his again, shock widening them to impossible proportions. 'You?' she whispered, and then swallowed hard, recovering her composure with visible effort. 'We'll be working together, then,' she added in a commendably normal voice. 'I'm your registrar.'

'My registrar?'

It was his turn to sound shocked. As his registrar, she'd be working with him on a daily basis, and he'd be intimately involved with every aspect of her training. Ruthlessly he crushed the surge of delight and tried to restrain his smile.

'So we'll be working together,' he said, stating the obvious.

'Apparently.'

'Have you two worked together before, then?' David Armstrong interrupted again.

'No. We, ah, met each other on holiday. Only briefly, a little over a year ago. I don't think we got round to surnames.'

Annie made a tiny strangled noise and looked frantically around her. 'Oh, look at the time! I have to get on—we've got a list and I'm assisting the Specialist Registrar. Unless you want to take over?'

He looked back down at her, her wide, green eyes guarded now, and his heart thumped again. 'No. You go ahead. I might pop in, but I've got a bit of orienteering to do before I can start work, and I think someone's kindly scheduled me a clinic for this afternoon. How about lunch?'

Panic fluttered in her eyes, and he hurried to reassure her. 'We ought to talk about work—I could do with you filling me in on what's what.'

The panic retreated, replaced by a faint wave of colour in her pale cheeks. 'Um—sure. OK. Whatever. I'll see if the SpR can come too. I'll bleep you when we've finished in Theatre.'

'Don't bother. I'll come up when I'm done.'

She nodded, then glanced up at the clock again. 'I really do have to get on.'

'OK. I'll see you. Which theatre?'

'Four. Someone will direct you.'

She had to go past him, but they were standing in a bottleneck by the nursing station and she brushed against him, sending heat through him again like a flash fire. He almost groaned aloud.

Working with her was going to be a very interesting experience. He just wasn't sure he'd survive it!

Of all the people, in all the places…!

Annie walked down the ward in a daze, her feet on autopilot. She picked up the notes, spoke to the patients she was due to see in Theatre shortly, reassuring them automatically as she went round the ward, but all the time her thoughts were on Max.

She'd always thought she wouldn't see him again, and yet now here he was—and not only here, but here for good, working with her, for heaven's sake! Suddenly everything seemed unbearably complicated.

She turned towards the ward door, ready to make

her escape, and he was there, hovering near the exit, in conversation with the charge nurse. As she approached he glanced up, his eyes spearing her so that her footsteps faltered.

'Excuse me,' he murmured to Damien, and then he was at her side, falling into step beside her. 'Change of plans,' he announced. 'The SpR has just phoned in sick, so I'm coming up to Theatre with you and you can fill me in as I work—or I can assist, if you like. I'd like to see you operate and there's no time like the present.'

She nearly choked. The consultant, assisting her? Oh, well, it might come in handy. One of the cases was promising to be a bit more tricky than they'd first expected and she had half anticipated that Steve Kelly, the SpR, would have to call the consultant, whoever he was. But—Max?

'Oh, well, you can always pick up the pieces,' she said, striving for a light note, but her heart was pounding and she felt an absurd mixture of elation and dread that was nothing to do with work and everything to do with this man striding along beside her on long, lean legs, charisma pouring off him like a tidal wave.

So many complications.

Well, no. Only one, really, but such an important one. Too important for her to allow her personal feelings to get in the way. Annie slid a sideways glance at his hand, but there was no wedding ring. That meant nothing, of course. Many doctors didn't wear one, particularly surgeons because of trapping germs under them or catching them on things. She always took her ring off for surgery and, in fact, for the last few weeks hadn't worn it at all.

Not that it counted now, really.

Passing through a doorway with Max's arm brushing hers and sending heat shooting through her body, she wondered if it had counted before, or if her role as Peter's wife had just been a part she'd played.

In which case, Max had definitely been a walk-on, walk-off one-liner.

But what a line!

'—on the list?'

'Sorry?'

'I said, can you fill me in on what's on the list? Who are we expecting?'

She dragged her mind back to the subject. 'Um…reversing a colostomy, laparoscopy for investigation of vague abdominal pain that might be almost anything, a hernia—I can't remember the other two.'

Not surprisingly. She could hardly remember her name. She tried to focus her thoughts. 'The laparoscopy might be complicated. She's got a chequered history.' She filled him in as they walked towards Theatre, but her mind was hardly on it. All she could think about, all she could see or hear was Max beside her, his rangy, well-muscled body, the slight scent of his soap and skin, remembered from that brief encounter—

Annie nearly choked, stumbling slightly on the perfectly level floor, and his hand came up like lightning to steady her elbow.

'All right?'

No! She was far from all right. She dredged up a

smile and detached herself from him. She couldn't allow this again. He must be married now, probably with a baby on the way.

'How's Fiona?' she asked, to remind him of his obligations so that one of them, at least, would remember that they had some, but he just gave her a slightly quizzical smile.

'Fiona? I imagine she's all right. She's married to a barrister now, living in London. I haven't seen her for over a year.'

Annie was sure her jaw dropped. Fiona, *married*? *To someone else?* She felt a little surge of something that could have been hope, and suppressed it ruthlessly. So what if he was free? She wasn't. Not truly. She had obligations, responsibilities.

So does he, her alter ego reminded her, but she ignored it. Only if she involved him would her obligations affect him, and she wasn't sure she could do that. Wasn't sure she dared. And anyway, there might be someone else in his life. Probably was. Bound to be.

Whatever, now was not the time. She slapped open the door to Theatre with the palm of her hand and breezed through it, smiling at everyone with everything except her eyes. 'Morning, all. This is our new consultant...'

Annie floundered, suddenly realising that she couldn't introduce him by his first name and she still didn't know his surname. How ridiculous, after all that had passed! She looked to him for help, but he was there already, smiling and holding out his hand.

'Williamson—Max Williamson. Good to meet you all.'

He shook hands with the theatre crew—the scrub nurse, Moira, the circulating nurse Annie thought was called Angie, Dick the anaesthetist. They merged into a blur and all smiled and joked and chatted while she stood there and suppressed her irrational urge to burst into tears or scream.

What on earth was she going to do? She couldn't work with him every day and not tell him, it wasn't in her nature, but—hell's teeth, what a can of worms!

'Right, I'm going to scrub. We've got the first coming up in about ten minutes.'

They all looked at her as one, and she realised her crisp voice had sliced through their banter and brought a slightly shocked silence to the room. She offered a tentative smile and fled to the changing room.

Annie was nervous, not surprisingly. Max remembered operating in front of his consultant for the first time, and he could distinctly recall the adrenaline rush and the wild urge to hyperventilate.

He smiled at her, but his mask was in the way and, anyway, she wasn't looking at his eyes. Anywhere else but, he thought, and gave a quiet sigh. She was married. Their brief meeting had been an aberration, a very short-lived hiccup in the even tenor of her life. He could hardly expect her to look at him with devotion, even if she had, once, for just a few very short hours.

He forced himself to concentrate on her hands, and noticed they were trembling.

'Take your time,' he said quietly. 'Nice light, smooth strokes with the scalpel. Don't fidget with it—

that's lovely. Bit more, give yourself room to move. Better. OK. Now the next layer.'

He cauterised a tiny vessel and the scrub nurse swabbed to keep the field clear so she could see what she was doing, and gradually she relaxed into her work.

She was good, he had to admit. A natural. There were things she needed to learn, but she had the ability in her to be a very good surgeon. Not everybody did, no matter what their inclination. It took more than just the desire to be a surgeon to make you into one.

The patient was having a colostomy reversed after a section of bowel had been rested to heal the ulceration and perforation following neglected diverticular disease, so she told him. Now, a few weeks after the initial operation, the end of the bowel that had been brought out onto the abdomen to form an outlet was being reattached to the recovered lower part of the bowel, and once healed should restore normal function and dignity to the patient.

Provided, of course, that a correct diet and treatment regime was followed and the patient didn't stoically and erroneously struggle on regardless if it flared up again.

Under his supervision and instruction she performed the whole operation faultlessly, and he had the feeling she was simply tolerating his running commentary and knew exactly what to do anyway.

Fortunately she couldn't see his self-deprecating smile under the mask—or maybe unfortunately. If she only ever looked at him it would be an improvement, but maybe this was the way it had to be.

With a sigh he stepped back from the table and snapped off his gloves as he left the room, throwing them and the gown and mask into the bin and heading for the coffee-machine. She'd finished closing and was just swabbing the patient down, and she didn't need him any more.

He scrubbed a hand through his hair and sighed again. She never had needed him. He'd just been a moment's amusement, a little diversion to take her out of the humdrum routine of her marriage. Hell's teeth, it had only been one day, for goodness' sake! Hardly anything, really, except for the last brief hour that had changed the carefully orchestrated course of his life.

And it was more than obvious to him now that she wanted to forget it, to move on and leave the past behind, where it belonged.

Fine. That suited him. He had to work with her, and it was probably easier this way—or it would be, if his body would only take the hint and leave him alone. But it remembered her, the feel of her skin, the touch of her hands, the soft fullness of her breasts pillowed against his chest—

With a growl of frustration he smacked the coffee-cup down on the worktop, splashing his hand. He stared at it, watching the dark liquid dribble over his skin and catch on the fine hairs across the back of his knuckles. Would he never stop wanting her? Never stop remembering that day?

He heard her voice as she came out of the operating room, talking to one of the nurses. She was laughing, but it sounded dutiful to his ears.

Crazy. He didn't, surely, know her well enough to

know if she was truly amused or simply being polite? And then he turned and met her eyes, and they were anguished, and he knew that she remembered too, and was tormented by it.

He should have felt better, but instead he just felt sad, because nothing had really changed. She was still married, and still off limits, whatever had happened in his life.

He washed his hands and poured himself another coffee, retreating with it to a chair. There were plenty of seats. It would be interesting to see if she joined him.

She didn't. She sat instead with the nurses, and Dick, the anaesthetist, came and chatted to him about his previous experience and preferred methods of working. It should have interested him, but he found his ears tuned to every word Annie said.

Impatient with himself, he went into Recovery and checked their last patient, then scrubbed for the next case. A simple hernia, something he could have done with one hand behind his back, and Annie certainly didn't need him breathing down her neck. He assisted without a word, and she managed perfectly.

The next case, however, was different. Their patient had a history of grumbling pain and intermittent symptoms of obstruction, but there was no pattern that pointed to anything particularly and he doubted that they would see anything with this investigation that the plethora of other tests and investigations hadn't revealed.

While the operating room was being cleaned and prepared, he went through the notes, checking the results of the bloods and all the less invasive tests that had been done.

Nothing. Not a hint, not a clue. That was bad news. He didn't have a single idea what they were looking for. Lots of possibilities, but most of them could be dismissed by the lack of evidence to support them. It could be anything or nothing, and they wouldn't know until they had a look inside.

Still, at least it would make him concentrate, unlike the last case where he'd had nothing to do but look at Annie's hands and imagine them on his body...

She was glad Max was there. The tiny spot of endometrial tissue on the woman's bowel wall was so small she would have missed it, especially as she wasn't looking for a gynaecological cause for the pain.

'I think that's our problem,' he murmured, pointing it out on the monitor screen, and with a simple touch of the laser he zapped it into a puff of smoke and straightened up, flexing his shoulders.

She stared at them, fascinated. They were broad and solid, and she could remember the feel of them under her hands.

'I wouldn't have found that,' she said honestly, dragging her mind back to their patient.

'Yes, you would, if you'd kept an open mind. You just have to think, What hurts? Endometriosis hurts, often without an obvious menstrual pattern, particularly if the periods are irregular. Did anyone check for that?'

She shrugged. 'I don't know. I wasn't involved with

her case,' she confessed. 'Will you refer her to Gynae for follow-up?'

'Maybe. She might not need it. We'll see how she is in a few weeks. Fancy closing?'

She didn't. She wanted to watch his strong, capable hands, but that was stupid.

'Sure,' she murmured, and took over from him. He left the room, and she felt the tension drain out of her body.

Only two more to go and she could escape, she told herself, and then remembered she was having lunch with him.

Working lunch, she reminded herself, but a little frisson of something that could have been anticipation danced over her skin. You're an idiot, she scolded herself as she stitched her patient. He's your boss.

Whatever he'd been before—and she still didn't really know what he had been, apart from incredibly disturbing to her peace of mind, and a long-cherished memory—he was now her boss, and she had to keep her relationship with him impersonal and professional.

She had to, there was no choice. There was too much at stake, and she couldn't afford to play games, however tempting.

Always assuming, of course, that he even wanted to play games with her. Maybe he regretted their little fling—gracious, had it even been long-lived enough to be called a fling? Maybe he had put it behind him.

If so, she envied him. She'd found it impossibly difficult to forget him, and hadn't even tried. It was only the thought of him that had kept her going over the past incredibly difficult months, a constantly running loop of memory—his touch, his laughter, the tenderness in his eyes, the heat of his kiss.

She straightened up from the patient and handed her back to the anaesthetist with a strained smile. 'She's all yours, Dick,' she said, and left the room. With any luck Max would have taken himself off for a while, or be in Recovery, she thought, but luck was against her.

He was there, standing by the coffee-machine with a thoughtful look on his face, and as he turned his head and met her eyes, it was just like it had been the first time…

CHAPTER TWO

IT WAS a glorious May evening, but Annie was filled with a restless tension. She and Peter had spent the day walking the fells, following a carefully planned route with Peter referring to the map every other minute with almost religious fervour.

'It looks lovely up there,' she'd said at one point, but he'd dismissed it.

'But we're not going that way,' he'd said, and had headed off on a different path towards his chosen objective. And, of course, it had been probably just as lovely when they'd got there, but it hadn't been spontaneous, and Annie longed, just once, to do something spontaneous and unplanned.

And then, when they'd almost got back at the car, he'd stumbled on a loose rock and had turned his ankle, and they'd had to sit by the path for a few minutes until the pain had subsided. Eventually he'd limped back down to the road, aided by the stout support of his walking boots and her shoulder to lean on, and she'd run on ahead and brought the car to him to save him the extra hundred yards or so.

Now they were sitting on the hotel terrace overlooking the lake, basking in the warmth of the evening sun, and Peter had his foot propped up on another chair and was staring at it morosely.

'Do you want to go to A and E?' Annie asked him for the fourth time, but he shook his head.

'For heaven's sake, Anne, stop fussing. I'm a doctor. I know what's wrong with it. I've strained the darned thing, that's all. It'll be fine by the morning.'

She didn't agree, but there was no reasoning with him, so she gave up and sipped her gin and tonic and let the beauty of the evening soak into her. She closed her eyes and turned her face up to the sun, and gradually the tension and frustration seeped away.

The air was awash with sounds—Peter's newspaper rattling, the whisper of the wind in the trees, the song of the birds. A car drove into the car park, and she listened idly to the voices in the distance and the crunch of gravel underfoot as they approached.

'I am *never* doing that again,' a woman's voice said with a touch of petulance. 'I hurt from end to end, my feet are raw, my legs ache—I need a drink. This had better be a good hotel.'

'It's an excellent hotel,' a deep, rich voice assured her, and Annie opened her eyes and looked across the terrace.

It was the man in his well-worn jeans and battered boots that caught her eye first. He was tall and broad, with the lithe, athletic grace of a natural sportsman, and he moved easily, making nothing of the weight of the big cases. Limping beside him in stark contrast was a slim blonde in designer jeans and brand-new boots that seemed to be giving her hell, and she was passing it all on to her unfortunate companion. She was clearly as mad as a wet hen, and Annie suppressed a smile.

They disappeared inside and she closed her eyes again, resting back against the seat and idly sipping her drink.

'I don't think walking's her thing,' she murmured to Peter, and he grunted.

'Not used to it, obviously. Bit silly to try, really, when you aren't fit enough.' He grunted again, this time with pain, and she opened her eyes and looked at him.

He was flexing his ankle, and he looked pale. She opened her mouth, met his eyes and shut it. He was a doctor. If he wanted to go to A and E, he'd say so. Always the worst patients, she told herself, and drained her glass.

'Fancy another drink?'

He shook his head. 'No. I'm saving myself for the wine with dinner, but you go ahead if you want.' He managed to make her sound like a lush, but in truth she didn't like the sort of wine that he enjoyed, the heavy, smoky reds flavoured with oak. She preferred light, fruity wines, but he dismissed them and tried to educate her, and she put up with it because it was easier than arguing with him.

It was always easier to give in and pretend, but tonight she didn't feel like giving in. 'I want one,' she said with a touch of defiance, and stood up, scooping up her glass from the table and heading through the door.

It opened as she reached it, and the man with the disgruntled companion paused on the threshold and held it for her.

She looked up to thank him, and her breath jammed

in her throat. What amazing eyes! Pale grey-blue, with navy rims, shot through with sparks of gold and cobalt. Astonishing eyes, beautiful eyes, rimmed with dark lashes and creased at the corners from laughter.

He smiled now, the crow's-feet crinkling, and her heart crashed against her ribs. 'Thank you,' she murmured, and stepped through the doorway beside him. He glanced towards Peter, who was prodding his ankle and frowning.

'Has he hurt himself?'

She looked back over her shoulder and sighed. 'Yes—he's twisted his ankle. He won't go to A and E.'

'Want me to look at it? I'm a doctor—I could save you a journey, maybe.'

'Thanks for the offer, but you can relax. We're both doctors, too. He won't let you look at it. He won't let *me* look at it, and I'm his wife!' She held out her hand and smiled. 'I'm Annie, by the way.'

'Max.' He took her hand, and heat engulfed her body. Was it her imagination, or did he hold her hand just a second too long? Whatever, it seemed to last for ever and be over much too soon.

Releasing her, he straightened up and slanted her a crooked, mischievous grin. 'Better go. Fiona's waiting for her suitcase, and she's cross enough as it is. We'll see you later, maybe—and if you want me to have a look at that foot, just holler. You never know, a stranger and all that.'

She smiled back, wondering a little wildly if he could hear her heart beating against her ribs. 'Thank you,' she managed, and he went out, the door closing softly behind him.

She stood there for a moment gathering her scattered thoughts, then went through to the bar and ordered another gin and tonic and a few ice cubes in a sandwich bag for Peter's ankle.

'Would you like the menu outside, or are you coming in?' the waitress asked with a smile.

'Oh—thanks, I'll take it out.'

A door clicked, and the hairs shivered on the back of her neck. She knew without turning round that Max had just crossed the hallway and gone upstairs to Fiona the Furious.

His wife? Lucky woman, she thought idly, and checked herself. Peter was a good husband—if a trifle dull and set in his ways. At least he wasn't out running round playing the field like so many men these days. She couldn't abide that. There was no excuse for infidelity.

She went back out to him, her safe, predictable, regimented husband, and gave him the menu. 'Looks good tonight,' she commented, reading it over his shoulder.

The waitress, Vicky, arrived at her side. 'Any thoughts?'

Peter shut the menu. 'Yes. We'll both have the starter, then the sorbet instead of the soup, and then the lamb, I think. It'll go nicely with that red we didn't finish last night. We might have another bottle—although there was an interesting little Rioja—'

'Count me out,' Annie said hastily. 'I'll have a glass

of whatever white Hans recommends—I fancy the salmon in the filo parcel.'

Peter looked at her as if she'd lost it. 'You aren't having the lamb? You like lamb.'

'Mmm. I like salmon, too.' And I don't like red wine, she added silently to herself.

'One lamb, one salmon and a glass of whatever Hans suggests. Righty-ho.' Vicky scooped up the menu, put a little plate of canapés down in front of them and disappeared back inside, leaving them alone in a slightly shocked silence.

Annie waved the sandwich bag at Peter before he could start. 'I brought you some ice, by the way, for your ankle, and you know that couple who arrived a minute ago? He's a doctor. He offered to have a look at it for you.'

'I hope you told him it wouldn't be necessary,' Peter said with a touch of asperity, and she sighed to herself.

'I told him we were doctors, too,' she conceded, and laid the ice carefully over the swollen joint. 'It looks puffier.'

'It's fine.'

She gave up. She wasn't his mother, after all. She sat down again, staring out over the lake and sighing with contentment. 'It's beautiful here.'

He looked at the lake consideringly. 'Yes.' He sounded almost surprised, as if beauty in the Lake District was an afterthought. His gaze dropped to his foot. 'I wonder what this is going to be like in the morning? I don't suppose it'll be up to climbing, but maybe with a boot on it'll feel different. We were going to do the walk up from Wasdale Head, but I think that might be a bit of a challenge for it. We might need to rethink.'

He sounded shocked at the thought, and she smothered a smile. 'Why don't we think about it tomorrow?' she suggested soothingly. 'There's no hurry.'

'Well, I suppose…'

She heard the crunch of gravel and glanced up, straight into those amazing eyes. 'Max,' she said with a spontaneous smile, and turned to Peter. 'This is the doctor I was telling you about. We met briefly in the doorway—and you must be Fiona. I'm Annie, and this is my husband, Peter.'

Fiona smiled graciously enough, but her smile had a chilling quality, a sort of icy dismissal that absurdly made Annie cross. 'How nice to meet you,' she said, but her words were shallow platitudes.

'Excuse me if I don't get up,' Peter said with a grimace at his foot. 'I've done something stupid.'

Max nodded. 'Yes, I gathered, from Annie. Well, if you'd like me to look at it, I'm more than happy—'

'That won't be necessary, but thank you anyway,' Peter told him a little shortly. Then, perhaps conscious of his less than friendly tone, he invited them to pull up a chair.

'Thanks, we will,' Max agreed with alacrity, and Annie wondered if he didn't want to be alone with his cross fiancée and her sore feet. 'So, where were you walking when this happened?' Max asked conversationally, settling into a chair and waving his glass at Peter's foot.

'Oh, round the back of Blencathra. Silly accident,

really. It was all my own fault. Had a good day yourselves?'

Fiona snorted quietly, and Max pulled a wry face. 'Fiona and I don't see eye to eye about hill walking,' he said with what was evidently masterly understatement.

'I just don't see the point in going up all that way to see a view when you can walk into a shop in Keswick or Windermere and buy a postcard!' Fiona said with a thread of irritation still touching her well-modulated voice. 'Or buy a book, if you really want to lash out. I'm sure there are tons of them.'

'I'm sure there are, but it's cheating,' Max said. 'And anyway, photos don't smell of peat and heather and salt from the sea, and you can't feel the tug of the wind and the moisture in the air and the sun on your back—it's just not the same.'

'No, it doesn't hurt, and you don't get sheep's muck on your bottom when you sit down!' Fiona retorted. 'And as for that lunatic drive over that pass—well!'

Max rolled his eyes and leant back in his chair with a chuckle. 'I give up,' he said, and turned to Peter. 'I gather we're in the same line of business,' he said, changing the subject.

'So I understand. I'm a consultant physician in Bristol.'

Max wrinkled his nose. 'I don't have the patience for that, I like quicker results. I'm a surgeon—I'm working in London at the moment.' He turned to Annie and smiled, and her heart thumped for some ridiculous reason. 'And you? Are you still practising, or are you a lady of leisure like Fiona?'

She laughed a little ruefully. 'No such luck. I'm just finishing off a gynae rotation, for the next few weeks at least, and then I've got a job as a surgical registrar. I feel the same as you—I like to go in and sort things out, not fiddle around with drugs and wait three months to see that there hasn't been any change and try again!'

'I can't imagine why any of you want to poke around in other people's bodies! I think It's all a bit odd, really,' Fiona said with a delicate shudder. 'Still, I suppose when you're in Harley Street, darling, it won't be so bad.'

Max arched a brow expressively, his mouth twitching. 'What, because they'll be rich bodies? And anyway, as I keep telling you, I don't want to work in Harley Street.'

Another well-worn argument, Annie thought, and wondered what he saw in her. Maybe in London their differences were less exaggerated, but certainly here, in the raw beauty of the Lakes, they seemed like chalk and cheese.

Rather like her and Peter, she thought in astonishment, seeing their relationship clearly for perhaps the first time. He was talking to Fiona, drawing her out with extraordinary ease, and Annie guessed it was because she was on her favourite subject—herself. Max caught her eye and winked, and she smiled slightly, wondering why her heart should hiccup like an adolescent's every time he looked at her.

And then Vicky came and rescued her, escorting them slowly to their table with Peter wincing every step of the way. Max and Fiona were shown in a few minutes later, but their table was on the other side of the room and Annie couldn't see them without turning her head.

She was aware of Max, though, curiously aware, every murmur of his voice finding its way to her ears. Once he laughed, a low, soft sound that sent shivers down her spine, and she totally lost the thread of her conversation with Peter.

They didn't stay downstairs for coffee. Peter's foot was troubling him, and so they decided to have an early night. The following morning his ankle was more swollen, to his great disgust, and he had to abandon his plans for the walk.

They went down for breakfast, and met Max and Fiona in the dining room. She was protesting, yet again, at the prospect of having to walk so much as another step, and she turned to Annie and Peter as they went in, latching onto them like a lifeline.

'Look, Peter obviously can't go either, so why don't you and Annie go for a walk somewhere and Peter and I'll just sit here and have coffee and chat? How about it, Peter?'

'What a good idea,' he agreed before Annie could intervene. 'We'll be fine here, and it seems a shame for you to have to abandon your plans to walk just because of my stupid ankle, Anne. Max, what do you think?'

Max was looking at Annie with a curiously veiled expression in his eyes. 'Yes, sure, if Annie's in agreement.'

And Annie found herself outmanoeuvred by all of them. To refuse would have seemed churlish, and in truth she didn't really know why she wanted to refuse, but she had a strange feeling somewhere between excitement and dread that made her veins tingle and her heart race.

She realised they were all waiting for her reply and, defeated, she lifted her shoulders in a little shrug of submission. 'Fine,' she said.

And that was that. Half an hour later, she found herself walking up the drive with Max, heading for the hills behind the hotel. They left the cars with Fiona and Peter, and set off at a brisk pace, falling naturally into step with each other. He adjusted his stride to hers automatically, something Peter would never have done, and then as they reached a fork in the path, he turned to her with a grin.

'Which way?' he asked.

She was astonished. 'Haven't you planned it?' she said.

He chuckled. 'Planned it? No. I've got a map here somewhere, but it's probably got a coffee stain right in the middle of the bit we want. So, lady, left or right?'

She looked around her, suddenly filled with a great surge of freedom, and laughed. 'Right,' she said firmly, and he nodded.

'Right it is. Do you want to go first, or follow me?'

'Can I go first? I hate not being able to see the track.'

'Sure.'

So she led the way, and they climbed high up Helvellyn and looked back down on Thirlmere, with the dam at the northern end and Grasmere away to the south and the sea in the distance, and she laughed again with the wonder of being alive.

'You sound happy.'

'I am. It's so nice just to walk—not have to follow a map and make sure you're on the exact path, and go at a set speed.'

'Peter, I take it?'

She sighed and lifted her hair off her nape. It was damp with the effort of the climb, and she savoured the cooling breeze for a moment. 'Yes, Peter. He likes things…ordered.'

'And you don't.'

'Not everything. He can't do anything off the cuff—he has lists. I don't know, sometimes I think he makes love to me because it's on his list—'

She broke off, shocked that she'd said anything so personal—so disloyal—to a total stranger, but he didn't feel like a stranger. He felt like a friend, someone who intuitively understood her. Even so…

'I'm sure he doesn't,' Max said softly. 'I'm sure even the worthy Peter would find a better reason than that.'

She looked up swiftly and met his eyes, and realised it was a compliment. She looked away, confused by the sudden surge in her pulse and the heat that raced through her. 'He's a good man,' she said defensively. 'I shouldn't have said that, it was unfair.'

'Nobody's talking about fair. Sometimes you just need to get things off your chest, and I get the feeling you don't do that very often.'

'I don't,' she admitted. 'You're right, I bottle things up.'

He plucked an ear of grass and removed the seeds one by one, giving it far more attention than it deserved. 'Why did you marry him?' he said after a moment, and she blinked.

'Why? I don't know. Because I loved him?' Did he notice her use of the past tense? He didn't comment, if so, just moved on.

'Security? He's older than you, isn't he?'

It wasn't really a question. It was obvious he was older than her, much older, whereas Max was probably only thirty or so, just three or four years her senior. 'He's thirty-eight. I'm twenty-seven. We've been married two years.'

'And were you flattered by his attention?'

Annie sighed and pulled up a blade of grass, shredding it systematically. There was going to be none left at this rate. 'Flattered? Probably. He's very kind.'

'I don't doubt it. He's also exceedingly dull—he's like an entomologist. If I look closely I'll probably find a pin through your heart.'

She laughed, a little hollow sound that was whisked away on the wind. 'And what are you going to do—set me free?'

'For now, at least.'

Their eyes met and locked, and Annie had a strange and inexplicable urge to cry.

'We ought to get back,' she said, guilt tugging at her, but she didn't want to.

'Come on,' he said softly, and pulled her to her feet. 'We'll go down the long way.'

It was harder going down than coming up, and they stopped halfway to rest their legs for a minute. In the distance they saw a car turn out of the hotel drive, and Max shaded his eyes and peered at it more closely.

'That looked like my car. Maybe Fiona's decided to buy one of her postcards.'

'Tell me about her,' Annie said impulsively.

'Fiona? I thought she did a good job of that herself last night.'

'No, I mean the two of you. You seem...'

'Different?' He smiled ruefully. 'You might say that.'

'She's not really much for the great outdoors, is she?'

'No.' He sighed. 'She keeps talking about Harley Street, and I think she really believes I'll end up there. Nothing could be further from the truth. I want to live somewhere where I can go for walks and be near the sea—I've got a boat, nothing flashy but it's fun. It's a sailing boat and it goes like a rocket, and she hates it. She hates anything smelly or dirty or risky.'

'She wouldn't like bowel surgery, then,' Annie said with a wry grin, and he laughed.

'Absolutely not.' He looked down at his feet, scuffing a stone idly. 'We're getting married in four weeks. Four weeks and two days, to be exact.'

'You don't sound thrilled,' she said cautiously, and he gave a brittle laugh and straightened up.

'No. Bit worrying, really, isn't it?' he muttered, and set off down the hill again. They walked the rest of the way in silence, and when they arrived back at the hotel it was to find that Peter and Fiona had gone out together.

'They said something about lunch in Keswick,' Hans told them.

Annie and Max exchanged glances. 'Fancy going out for lunch?' Max suggested, but she shook her head, guilty because she'd enjoyed herself more today with this stranger than she ever had with Peter—or ever would.

'We ought to be here, really, when they come back.'

'I could get you some lunch—perhaps a little picnic?' Hans said. 'Some chicken and fruit, a bottle of wine? We've got a small rowing boat—you could take it out on the lake and have a picnic. You'd be here, then. We could shout for you.'

Annie looked up at Max, wondering if her face reflected the wistful hope in her heart despite the guilt. 'It sounds fun.'

Max scanned her face thoughtfully, then turned to their host with a smile. 'Thank you, Hans, that would be lovely.' He turned back to Annie. 'Shall we shower first?'

She tugged at her damp T-shirt and laughed. 'Probably a good idea. It was hot, climbing up Helvellyn. I'll see you down here in a few minutes.'

It took her ten, including spending five minutes vacillating over her wardrobe. In the end she wore the soft wrapover skirt she'd had on last night, and a fresh T-shirt—nothing flirty or provocative or especially flattering, just normal clothes on what was starting to feel like a most un-normal day.

She hesitated over make-up, and settled for a swipe of lip balm. Then, suddenly inexplicably nervous, she ran downstairs to meet Max.

He was in the foyer, his hair damp from the shower, a covered basket dangling from one hand, a tartan rug slung over his shoulder. He was dressed in jeans and battered trainers and a T-shirt, and he looked lean and hard and good enough to eat. He smiled at her, and her heart flipped.

You're stupid. You're a married woman, she told herself, but she'd gone suddenly deaf to the voice of reason.

'All set?'

Annie nodded, and he opened the door. As she went past him into the sunshine, she caught the mingled scents of soap and clean linen and something wholly masculine that made her body yearn.

Ridiculous. She was being ridiculous, and she was going to embarrass herself in a moment. He was just passing the time, having a little fun with her, a mild, meaningless flirtation.

A path wound through bushes to the shore, and there on the stony beach was the little rowing boat Hans had told them about. Max pushed it into the water, helped her in with the basket and rug at her feet and pulled off his old trainers.

'This is going to be freezing,' he said with a grin, and rolling up his jeans to mid-calf he pushed off, jumping aboard as the boat moved away with the practised skill of a sailor.

He winked at her, pushed the boat out further with an oar and then rowed them out into deep water with a few powerful strokes. It was a joy to watch him move, his body fluid and supple, the muscles rippling under the fine cotton of his shirt.

They went south, following the shore on their left, until she spotted a tiny cove. She pointed it out to him, and he changed course and grounded the little boat on the beach, jumping out and gasping at the cold. 'Ye gods, I swear it's meltwater!'

'So we're not swimming, then?' she said with a chuckle.

'Don't get clever or I'll accidentally tip you in it,' he warned.

She grinned. 'I'm terrified.'

'You need to be. Come here.'

Warily she stood up and went towards him, the boat wobbling slightly in the water even though it was beached. He held out his arms and she grasped them at the shoulder, and then seemingly effortlessly he lifted her clear of the boat and set her down on the shore above the waterline.

Once the boat was dragged a little way up the beach, he picked up the picnic basket and rug and looked around. 'Up here?'

She followed the direction of his gaze and saw a little glade in the trees, dappled with sunshine, the grass mossy and sweet. It was breathtakingly perfect and unbelievably romantic, and her heart started to beat slowly and heavily against her ribs.

'Fine,' she said casually.

He spread the rug out and sat on it, patting it to beckon her to join him. She knelt down and peered curiously into the picnic basket, desperate for a safe topic.

'What is there?'

He pulled the contents out—a couple of chicken

legs, some smoked salmon sandwiches, sliced fruit in a bowl and a small bottle of a delicate dessert wine. Wrapped in a cloth were two glasses and a corkscrew, and he whipped the cork out with a flourish and poured the wine, handing her a glass.

She sniffed it cautiously, then tasted it, and sighed with delight. 'It's gorgeous. It isn't sickly at all, but it's just bursting with fruit.'

'That's Hans. I left it up to him. Come on, eat up.'

She needed no second bidding. The walk had made her hungry, and probably thirsty, too, because she found herself drinking a second glass of the deliciously fruity wine as they laughed and talked about nothing in particular. Then Max scooped up the last little sliver of melon and fed it to her, his fingers brushing her lips and setting them on fire.

She froze, her breath locked in her lungs, and with a slight shake of his head he got to his knees and cleared away the debris into the basket. He wasn't looking at her—anywhere but, it seemed. Something had happened, some sudden shift in their relationship, and without thought of the consequences she reached out a hand and touched his arm.

'Max?'

He turned his head then, his eyes burning with a brilliant cobalt fire in their icy depths. 'You've got juice on your lips,' he told her gruffly. Reaching for a napkin, he blotted gently at her mouth, staring at it with curious intensity.

'Is it gone?' she asked a little unsteadily.

He didn't reply. The flame flickered in his eyes, and she swallowed hard. They were kneeling face to face, just inches apart, and she was headily conscious of the scent of his body and the rise and fall of his chest so near her own.

'Max?' she whispered.

'God forgive me, but I have to do this,' he said under his breath, and with a fractured sigh he lowered his head and kissed her.

His lips were firm but soft, their touch like the stroke of an angel's wing, and she was powerless to resist. He tasted of fruit and wine and sunshine, and with a little cry she leant into him and kissed him back.

For a second he was motionless, but then he groaned and gathered her up into his arms, wrapping her against his chest and plundering her mouth with his, and she was lost.

She gave him everything she had, everything she was, everything she could be, and he took it with infinite care and reverence and returned it tenfold, giving her a tenderness and passion she'd never imagined in her wildest dreams.

And when she fell apart in his arms he was there for her, with her, crying out her name as he stiffened against her, his arms tightening convulsively and cradling her against his chest as the tidal wave of sensation receded and left her emotions flayed raw by the strength of their passion.

'Max?' she said tremulously, and he soothed her, his hands gentling her, his words soft.

'It's OK, Annie. I've got you.'

'I didn't know,' she whispered. 'I had no idea—I didn't realise it could be so…'

She floundered to a halt, but he didn't need her words. He understood, his arms tightening again as he held her. 'Nor did I,' he admitted gruffly. 'Nor did I.'

His lips found her tears and kissed them away, and when she opened her eyes his lashes were clumped with tears of his own.

'We have to go back,' she said, her voice hollow with dread, and he nodded.

'I know.'

'I can't.'

'Yes, you can, and so can I. You can go back to your safe, reliable Peter who'll never get you lost, and I'm going to marry Fiona next month.'

'We can't see each other again,' she said, almost hoping he'd contradict her, but of course he didn't.

'No, we can't. This is all we have, all we'll ever have. Just one stolen moment to treasure—and I will treasure it, for ever,' he vowed.

She closed her eyes against the threatening tears, and he rolled away from her. She heard the rasp of a zip, the clink of glass as he shifted the picnic basket, the crunch of his footsteps as he walked down to the boat.

She dressed herself hastily, dragging on her serviceable and unseductive cotton knickers, straightening her skirt, her T-shirt, running her fingers through her hair to bring some sort of order to it. Her shoes were scattered, one under the edge of the rug, one lying on the grass feet away. She put them on, shook out the rug and folded it and looked around.

Apart from the slight flattening of the grass, there was no sign of their presence. Odd. She felt the ground should be permanently marked, scorched by the heat of the fire that had consumed them.

She went down to the boat and he lifted her in, then pushed off and rowed back to the hotel in a wordless silence. As they walked up the path they met Fiona coming towards them, and as she saw them she paused and threw up her hands.

'At last! Where on earth have you been? I've been bored to death—I've just spent the last two hours sitting in Casualty at the cottage hospital in Keswick waiting for Peter to be told he's got a broken bone, and he's in such a mood!'

Guilt gripped Annie, and she looked up at Max. 'I must go to him.'

'I'm sorry,' he said. 'If I can help…'

'Good heavens, it's only a tiny fracture,' Fiona said crossly. 'Max, I want to go somewhere civilised, an art gallery or something.'

'I'll change.'

'Well, hurry, because I'd like to go now.'

Annie left them to it, and ran into the hotel to find Peter sitting in the lounge with his foot propped up and Hans in attendance, pouring him a cup of tea.

'There you are! Anne, we have to leave,' he said, and she looked at his chalk-white face and felt the blood drain from her own.

'What is it?' she asked, and he ran a trembling hand over his face and met her eyes.

His own were bleak and expressionless. 'It's a pathological fracture—a metastatic carcinoma of the fibula.'

She sat down with a bump on the arm of the chair. 'Secondary bone cancer?' she whispered.

He nodded, and she swallowed hard. 'Oh, Peter—I'll pack.'

They left half an hour later, and she didn't see Max again. She'd remembered him, though, in a haze of guilt and recrimination, through the next four dreadful months until Peter's death from the hitherto almost silent primary growth around his aorta. And then afterwards, she'd clung to the memory of that one stolen moment to keep her sane through her pregnancy and the birth of her child.

Her beautiful daughter with eyes just like her father's—eyes like those searching her face now, pale grey-blue rimmed with navy, startling against the thick, black lashes and the shock of dark brown hair.

Max's child.

CHAPTER THREE

ANNIE looked so troubled. Max wanted to reassure her that he wasn't going to put the moves on her or try and pick up their relationship—huh, what relationship?—where they'd left off, but how could he bring the subject up, for heaven's sake?

Turning away from her, he scrubbed a hand through his hair and reached for another mug of coffee. 'Everything OK?' he asked casually, and she nodded.

There was no sign of her smile, that wide and uninhibited and totally mind-blowing smile that just did him in. He ached to see it again, but there was precious little sign of it this morning.

'So, what's next?' he asked, and wondered if they'd ever get to lunch.

'Um…I don't know without looking. I can't remember the order—'

Angie stuck her head round the door. 'Call from A and E—there's an RTA victim with a rigid abdomen coming up, very shocky, they've cross-matched and given him fluids but it looks like a major bleed.'

Max put the coffee down. This was it, then, his first test as a consultant, and all eyes would be on him to see how big a fist he made of it. The last thing he needed was too much caffeine so he couldn't think straight.

He snapped out instructions as the cleaners left the

theatre, everything sterile again and all the equipment replaced and ready. Dick was already at work on their patient in the anteroom, and moments later the young man was wheeled in and moved carefully to the table.

It was, predictably, a blood bath once they opened him up.

'His spleen's gone,' Max said unnecessarily. Sliding his hand inside, he groped in the mass of mangled tissue and found the splenic artery, cutting off its circulation. 'Right, get him sucked out, let's find out what else is leaking.'

It took only a few minutes to establish that for every leak they found and plugged, another one would pop up somewhere else. A nurse was bagging blood into him through two giving sets simultaneously, but they were hardly keeping pace. Then Max turned the liver over and found a split under the back of a lobe that was steadily leaking.

Muttering under his breath, he clamped it and stood watching for a moment. Nothing happened, and the tension in Theatre eased visibly.

'Finally,' he growled, and set about repairing the damage as fast as possible.

'The spleen's a goner,' he told them, thinking aloud. 'I think I can patch up the rest without a problem. I might try and leave part of it, just take the tail off. I hate knackering the immune system permanently if I can avoid it.'

It took over an hour from that point before the spleen was repaired to his satisfaction, and all the other little bits and pieces took another forty minutes. In all, they were two hours behind schedule as a result of the emergency, and that, of course, put paid to lunch and left him running late for his clinic.

Still, at least it had proved to him that his registrar was a valid and useful member of the team, and level-headed in an emergency. Always handy to know.

There were other things he needed to know about Annie, though, and things she needed to know about him—such as the fact that he didn't intend to let their past become an issue. All he needed was the chance to talk to her, and that was becoming increasingly difficult to fit in as the day went on.

Before he left the operating suite for his clinic, he showered rapidly and emerged from the changing room with his tie slung round his neck and his shirt buttons undone, shoving his shirt tails into his trousers, and he almost ran straight into her. Her hair was wet, her skin scrubbed and gleaming, and he had a desperate urge to kiss her.

No. Idiot.

'Annie, we need to talk,' he said without preamble, and she nodded and looked up at his face. Did he imagine it, or was there a touch of colour in her cheeks? And had she had to drag her eyes from his naked chest? He hauled the buttons together and she relaxed visibly. 'What are you doing after work?'

'Um, I'm busy,' she said, and her eyes slid away.

Peter, of course. 'Can you ring him? Tell him you'll be late? Or can we meet later?'

'Him?'

'Peter.'

She shook her head. 'It's not Peter.' She hesitated, then looked back at him, her eyes still wary and filled with doubt. 'But we do need to talk. Later—say, seven-thirty? I'll come to you. Where are you staying?'

'I've rented a house for a while—a little detached Edwardian place near the park. Will that do? Or do you want to go somewhere...?' Neutral, he'd been going to say, but changed it. 'Somewhere else? A pub? A restaurant? The park?'

She shook her head. 'Your house will be fine. Tell me the address,' she said, so he told her, and she nodded. 'OK. I'll see you there at half past seven.'

There was something curiously ominous about the way she said it that made his blood run cold. He watched her go, then gathered himself almost physically together and headed for his clinic. What a great start to his new career—over an hour late, and without time to look at any notes or prepare himself.

And all the time, in the back of his mind, was Annie...

'Darling, whatever's happened? You look as if you've seen a ghost!'

Annie scooped the baby out of her mother's arms and hugged her, kissing the wet, messy little face and laughing as her daughter clapped cereal-covered hands on her cheeks and giggled.

'You've just had your supper, haven't you? Have you been a good girl for your grannie?' she asked, but the baby just gurgled and laughed and pulled her hair with sticky fingers.

'She's been fine, haven't you, poppet? She went out with her grandad to the park, and fed the ducks, and had a lovely time. You, on the other hand, look as if you've been to hell and back. Want to fill me in while I clean her up?'

She handed little Alice back to her grandmother to have her face and hands de-cerealed, and took the opportunity to clean herself up. She licked her lips and frowned thoughtfully. 'Apple?'

'Apple and blackberry with millet flakes, and wizzerated roast chicken and vegetables from yesterday evening—and before you ask, yes, of course I reheated it thoroughly. There's tea in the pot, and we've run her bath, so bring it through to the flat and tell me all about it.'

Annie sighed. Her mother was nothing if not persistent, but there was no way she could tell her. Well, at least, not everything. Not *that*. She wouldn't understand, not that Annie herself really understood what had happened, or at least why it had, and there was no way she was going to upset the applecart unnecessarily now.

She poured herself a mug of tea, drank half of it and cleared up the kitchen, then topped up her tea and slowly, reluctantly followed her mother through to the little flat she shared with Alice in the garden wing of her parents' house.

She could hear giggling and shrieking from the bathroom and, smiling despite her mood, she went in and perched on the loo and watched them.

'She loves her bathtime with you,' Annie said wistfully, wishing not for the first time that she could be at home with her daughter, but there was no way she could afford the luxury. She had to finish her training and become a consultant before she had a hope even of working part time, and that process, of course, would take years.

Still, she was here now, and she pushed up her sleeves and knelt down by the side of the bath and joined in the fun.

Her mother shot her a thoughtful look, and Annie sighed inwardly. She knew that look. It meant her mother was just biding her time, and the Spanish Inquisition would start again shortly, just the moment Alice was settled for the night.

She had to avoid that—and she had the perfect excuse.

'I hate asking you, Mum, but could you put her to bed for me? I have to go out, and I need a shower. We had a blood bath in Theatre today and I really must scrub—and could I ask another favour? Could you babysit for me for a while? I won't be long, but I have to meet a new colleague at seven-thirty—we didn't get time today to do all we wanted, and I have to fill him in on things.'

She could almost hear the cogs turning and wished she'd left out the 'him'. Now her mother's maternal instinct was on red alert, and Annie's chances of avoiding that conversation indefinitely were slight in the extreme. If she put two and two together…

'Of course I'll put her to bed. You go ahead and get ready, and I'll keep an eye on her, it's no problem.' She lifted the protesting baby clear of the bathwater and swathed her in a huge, fluffy towel, and for a few moments there was silence.

Then her mother looked up and met her eyes. 'So,'

she said with an exaggerated disinterest that didn't fool Annie for a second, 'who is this man?'

Annie swallowed. 'His name's Max Williamson—he's the new consultant.'

Her mother's hands paused in the act of patting the baby dry, then resumed. 'I see.'

Annie hoped she didn't. She hoped her mother never saw—and never saw Max, because if she did, she'd know the truth, and Annie didn't know if her precious relationship with her beloved mother could bear the strain. If she knew she'd been unfaithful to Peter…

She looked away. 'I must get on. I'll get my things ready while you finish up in the bathroom. Don't bother to tidy it, Mum, I'll do it when I've finished.'

It was twenty past seven before she was ready, but that was fine. Max lived very close—too close for comfort, really, but at least it was an easy walk.

The doorbell rang dead on seven-thirty, and Max paused long enough to draw in a deep, steadying breath before walking slowly down the hall to open the door.

Annie looked lovely, of course—no make-up to speak of, but she didn't seem to wear it and frankly he didn't want her to, because her natural beauty was more than sufficient to knock him off his perch.

'Hi,' he said, holding the door for her, and she gave him a fleeting smile and crossed the threshold. A faint drift of something familiar caught his nostrils—her shampoo? Her perfume? Not obvious enough for perfume, but his body remembered the smell all too clearly.

'Fancy a drink?' he offered, scrabbling for common pleasantries and hoping he didn't disgrace himself absolutely.

'Um…thanks. Coffee? Tea?'

'Sure. Which?'

'Um…coffee.'

She seemed unsure of herself, something he could empathise with. He didn't know how to start this conversation, but then he reached out to turn on the kettle as she turned and they bumped into each other, and she recoiled with a tiny gasp.

That did it. He stepped back, closed his eyes briefly and opened them again to find her watching him warily.

'Annie, stop it,' he said tiredly. 'You're safe. I'm not going to jump on you. That's why I wanted to talk to you—just to tell you that it's all right. I'm not expecting us to pick up where we left off. Forget what happened, it's in the past. We can move on.'

For some reason her eyes clouded. 'Can we? I don't know that it's that simple—at least for me.'

What did she mean? It didn't matter. He didn't let himself think about it or try and work it out. Instead he just sighed and nodded. 'Yes, we can. We have to work together, and you've got Peter—'

'No.'

He searched her face carefully for clues, but there were none. 'No?' he said cautiously. 'Did you get divorced?'

She shook her head. 'He died.'

'Died?' He felt shock drain the blood from his face, and he leant back against the worktop and shook his head slowly. 'Oh, Annie, I'm so sorry.'

'No, don't be. Not for me. For Peter, maybe, but not for me. He was a good man, and I didn't deserve him.'

'That's rubbish.'

'No, it's the truth. Do you remember that fracture? Fiona took him to the hospital while we were...' She broke off, waving her hands as if searching for the words, then wrapped them tightly round her waist.

'Making love?' he offered softly.

Her eyes widened and she looked hastily away. 'It was a pathological fracture. He had cancer, Max. He died four months later.'

'Did you know?' he asked, a horrible thought creeping up on him unannounced and giving his voice a hard edge. 'Did you know about the cancer at the time?'

Her look speared him and he felt a wave of relief. 'Of course not! Do you really think I would have been gallivanting around the countryside with you if I'd had the slightest clue?'

He scrubbed a hand over his face and sighed. 'I'm sorry—sorry about all of it. How did you find out?'

'He knew then—that day. They'd told him at the hospital. That's why he was so moody with Fiona. He'd just been told he was dying, basically.'

Max nodded. 'Of course. They'd be able to tell it was a path. fracture in A and E. So where was the primary?'

'Round his aorta. He had chemo—it wasn't suitable

for surgery. He would have died instantly. It was right on the branch, behind his heart. It explained a lot, of course. Why he was so tired, why he had so much indigestion. It wasn't indigestion, of course, it was the tumour, but he didn't know that.'

Max turned away from her, resting both hands on the front of the worktop and dropping his head forwards against the wall cupboard. 'So you came back and had all sorts of tests and chemo and things, and he died—four months later, you said?'

'Yes.'

He sighed heavily. 'Annie, I really am so sorry if I added to your problems at the time.'

She made a sound that could have been a tiny, bitter laugh. 'In a strange way it was almost a help. At least my guilt gave me something else to think about and, of course, Peter was so shocked and so wrapped up in what was happening to him I don't think it occurred to him that we might have done anything.

'And then,' she continued with a wary edge to her voice, 'I discovered I was pregnant.'

Shock held him motionless for a second, then he turned slowly and met her steady, wounded eyes. 'Pregnant?'

She nodded. 'She's nearly eight months old now—her name's Alice.'

He hauled in a breath and the world seemed to right itself on its axis. 'Where is she now?'

'With my parents. I live with them, in a flat at the back of their house. Mum looks after her while I'm at work.'

She had a child. Peter's child, conceived—he ran

the maths through his head—before their holiday, about a month before. So she'd been pregnant with his child at the time…

He felt a sudden, raging jealousy that was totally irrational, and crushed it ruthlessly. There was no place in this for his feelings, none at all.

'Peter must have been very pleased,' he said in a neutral voice.

'He didn't know. I didn't until the day of the funeral, when I couldn't do up my skirt even though I'd lost weight. I couldn't understand it. It took my mother to explain to me.'

He nodded slowly. 'You must have been in shock. It must have been a hell of a time. I'm sorry.'

'You keep saying that.'

'Because it's the truth. What am I supposed to say? That I'm glad he's dead?'

'If it's the truth.'

'It isn't,' he said, surprised to find that he really meant it. What he'd hoped all along had been that she would have been able to walk away from him to Peter without a backward glance. He hadn't wanted the destruction of their marriage on his conscience—and he certainly hadn't wanted Peter's death.

But it did change things, potentially. If there was no one else in her life now, then maybe there was a chance for them.

He stared at his hands, wondering how to go on. 'Look, what I'd meant to say this evening about us picking up where we left off—as far as I was concerned you were married, albeit not apparently that happily, and I didn't want you thinking I was any threat to that.'

'And now?'

He shrugged. 'I don't know what to say. It all depends on you—how you feel.'

'I don't know how I feel,' she said honestly. 'Unsettled. I never thought I'd see you again. It all takes a bit of adjusting to.'

Her smile was crooked and very fleeting, but it lifted his heart.

'Ditto,' he said softly. 'Let's have some coffee and you can tell me all about it.'

'Nothing to tell,' she said. 'It was awful. To be honest, I just want to forget it.'

'So tell me about the baby.'

Annie's face softened. 'She's lovely. She's tiny, very dainty, and she's got a wonderful gurgling laugh and a passion for mashed bananas.'

He chuckled. 'What revolting taste.'

'She'd disagree with you.'

'No doubt. My nephews seem to eat the most disgusting combinations of things. I wouldn't be surprised to see them put ketchup on ice cream—but they're older, six and nearly eight. Black or white?'

'White, no sugar. Thanks.'

She took the coffee from him, carefully keeping her fingers away from his, and he picked up his mug and a packet of chocolate biscuits off the side and led her through to the sitting room.

'Sorry, the furnishings are a bit haphazard. Some of it's mine, some of it was here. That chair's comfortable.'

Max waved the chocolate biscuits towards his best chair, and she perched on the edge of it, cradling her coffee in both hands and looking thoughtful. He sat down on the lumpy old sofa and watched her, and after a moment she lifted her head and returned his gaze thoughtfully.

'Max, what happened with Fiona?' she asked a little diffidently, as if she felt she didn't have the right to ask, and he dredged up a smile.

'She met somebody else. After—that day, I realised I couldn't marry her.'

'Because of me?' She sounded shocked, and he smiled reassuringly.

'Because of me, I think, although you were definitely the catalyst. I just realised that day that I'd never had fun like that with Fiona, and I probably never would. And,' he continued quietly, looking down at his hands, 'making love to her became impossible. That night I pleaded tiredness, and then we returned to London and I found myself making excuses—working late, staying over at the hospital, even inventing emergencies.'

He tried for a smile, but it was wry and, no doubt, quite unconvincing. 'I probably should have realised she took it all too easily. Normally she would have thrown a paddy. As it was, she just accepted my excuses. Then about a week or ten days later, I told her I needed to speak to her. She said good, because she wanted to speak to me, too, and she told me she'd met someone else and wanted to marry him. And she did, on the day she should have married me.'

'The same day?' Annie said, sounding shocked, and he laughed softly.

'Oh, yes. The same wedding, in fact. Some of the presents went back, others were simply rebadged, as it were, and she married her London barrister. She wasn't going to give him a chance to change his mind, I don't think, and to be honest I think they're blissfully happy. Certainly she's happier than she would have been with me.'

'And you?'

He met her eyes, soft and mellow and tender in the muted light. 'What about me?' he asked a little gruffly.

'Are you happy?'

He thought of the endless nights spent longing for this beautiful woman sitting opposite him with her hair like burnished mahogany and eyes like a stormy sky. He thought of the images that had woken him, of the sweat and the aching and the need that had racked him. He thought of the times when he'd known she was in his arms, and had woken desolate to find it had just been another dream…

'I'll do,' he said a little crookedly.

'It's better than being trapped in the wrong marriage,' she murmured half to herself, and he realised she was talking about her marriage to Peter, a marriage that Max had sensed from the first had been a tragic mistake.

He didn't comment. There was nothing to say, nothing he had a right to say. She glanced at her watch and then looked up at him, and there was something evasive in her eyes. 'I have to go,' she said.

'I'll walk you to your car.'

'No—I don't have a car here. I walked.'

'Then I'll walk you home.'

Something that could have been panic flickered in her eyes and was gone. 'It's all right. Actually, I'm going somewhere else first. Do you mind if I call a taxi?'

'Annie, don't be silly. I'll drive you—'

'I'd rather you didn't. Really.'

And it dawned on him that she was going to visit a man, and naturally she wouldn't want him delivering her to his door. Jealousy speared through him again, and he leant back and pretended indifference.

'In that case, be my guest. The phone's beside you.'

He listened, but the address she gave as her destination meant nothing to him. The taxi took only a few minutes to come, but there was an awkward silence while they waited. He didn't want her to go, yet in a strange way he was relieved when she did.

He had a great deal to think about, and it was still a lovely evening, although it was dusk. He locked up the house and set off towards the park, then realised it would be shutting at dusk. Oh, well, he could walk round the streets instead, he thought, and, reaching the end of his road, he turned left and headed along the road beside the park. A taxi pulled up at the kerb ahead, and a woman got out and headed towards one of the big old houses facing the park.

A young woman who bore a striking resemblance to Annie.

He paused beside the wall, slipping quietly into the shadows until she was out of sight, then he walked on, his long stride covering the ground swiftly and silently until he came to the place where the taxi had stopped.

She stood in the well-lit porch of a big old Victorian house, and as the door opened she stepped inside.

It was her. He recognised her, even as he heard her say, 'I'm sorry, Mum, I forgot my key. Has she been all right?'

The door closed, leaving Max standing puzzled in the shadows. If she lived so close, why the taxi? And why say she was going on somewhere else? To make him jealous?

Unless she just didn't want him to know she lived so close to him. If he hadn't decided to go for a walk, he would never have known.

Bizarre. Why would she want to keep her whereabouts a secret, unless she didn't want him pestering her? If so, all she had to do was say so—and he'd hardly given her cause to think he was pestering her this evening, for heaven's sake!

Puzzled, confused and a little angry, he went back to his house, washed up the mugs and made himself another coffee, then sprawled in front of the television with the chocolate biscuits in one hand and the remote control for the television in the other, and channel-hopped his way through the late evening news.

He realised he'd been foolishly expecting her attitude to change ever since she'd told him about Peter, but why should it? So it was news to him. So what? It wasn't to her, and he'd already told her about Fiona earlier, so why should her attitude change? Obviously she'd decided she didn't need him. Well, that was fine. He didn't need her either.

He jabbed at the remote control viciously, plunging the set into silence, and with a harsh sigh he went upstairs, shed his clothes on the chair, visited the bathroom briefly and threw himself down on the bed with a disgusted snort.

'What did you expect, Williamson?' he asked himself shortly. 'Company?'

It would have been nice. Hell, it would have been more than nice, but he hadn't even so much as kissed her goodbye on the cheek!

He yanked the quilt over his legs, rammed a fist into the pillow and gave a grunt of disgust. No doubt his dreams would be Technicolored, as usual.

He closed his eyes, and all he could see was Annie's face, her eyes luminous against the alabaster of her skin. He pictured her body, her breasts swollen with milk, blue veins threading them as she suckled her baby, and desire slammed through him like an express train.

It was going to be a long, lonely night…

CHAPTER FOUR

BY THE following morning Max's emotions had settled down a little. He still didn't know why Annie hadn't told him where she lived, but the emotion that had filtered to the surface was hurt, pure and simple. He felt hurt that she hadn't trusted him. What did she think he was going to do? Pester her the entire time? Although, after his dreams, the thought was tempting…

He went to work a little warily, unsure quite how to approach her now, knowing what he did. As a result, he was a little distant, and he wasn't sure if he imagined it or if she seemed a little taken aback by that.

However, they were too busy to have time to worry. He had another outpatient clinic with Steve Kelly, the SpR, and during the course of it he had to go back to Theatre and open up the RTA victim they'd operated on the day before. He'd sprung another leak, and his pressure had been dropping steadily all morning.

Annie was in Theatre with him, and he let her perform the operation. Only a part of him was playing the tutor. The other part was a voyeur. He didn't really need to be there, in many ways. In an emergency he was quite confident that she could have coped without him, and he was beginning to realise that she could handle quite a high level of responsibility.

'I think you can manage on your own from now,' he said, and walked towards the door. 'I'm going to have a coffee. Give me a shout if you need a hand.'

He poured himself the last dregs from the coffee-machine and sat down on one of the plastic chairs, staring morosely into the murky liquid. He didn't really need the coffee. He'd had more than enough of it in the middle of the night while he'd been trying to escape from the images that had taunted him in the darkness. Even so, it was the lesser of two evils. The alternative was to stand and watch her, and that was probably even worse for him than the coffee.

Her head appeared round the door of the theatre. 'I think I've done it. Do you want to check? It was a leak in the mesenteric artery—I think it was weakened and just went during the night.'

Was it really necessary? New gloves, new mask, new gown, just to know that she had done it right. And if he didn't, and the man leaked again, he would have the responsibility for exposing him to yet another anaesthetic, more theatre time wasted and infinitely more expense. He put the mug down with a sigh and shrugged out of the chair.

'Can do.'

He didn't want to. She didn't need checking up on, he didn't suppose for a moment, but it was part of his job. He couldn't really understand his reluctance, and he realised he was letting his personal feelings get in the way of his professional judgement.

'You're a fool, Williamson,' he muttered to himself. 'Just a stupid, deluded fool.'

He realised he'd allowed himself to imagine that

things would be different now that he knew Peter was dead, but they weren't. Quite obviously, she had another man in her life, and even if she didn't, she'd made it abundantly clear last night by not letting him walk her home that she wasn't in the slightest bit interested in him. She had a child now, Peter's baby, and she had obviously moved on. It was only him that was fixated.

She had, of course, sutured the tiny rupture in the artery perfectly well, but he took the opportunity to check all his previous handiwork and make sure that there were no other possible areas that were going to give trouble before he left her to close.

'I'm going back down to the clinic now,' he said. 'Perhaps you could finish up here for me.'

He shouldered the door out of the way, stripping off his gloves and mask and gown as he went, and showered rapidly. Within five minutes, he was back down in his clinic, apologising profusely to all the patients he'd kept waiting.

Most of them were entirely reasonable, but there was always the odd one who felt they were different. He found his temper fraying, and realised it was nothing to do with his patients, simply a lack of sleep and the chaos that meeting Annie again had thrown him into.

He missed lunch. His clinic overran until nearly two, and then he had day-surgery cases all afternoon. As soon as he finished them, he went up to the ward to check on the previous day's patients and find out how their RTA man was getting on. He seemed fine, his pressure much better, a little groggy and in pain not unsurprisingly, but hopefully over the worst.

Damien Rayner, the charge nurse, seemed happy with his condition. He had him in a side ward under the eye of the staff constantly milling around the nursing station, and Suzie Crane was taking his obs every half-hour.

Max had half hoped that he would find Annie on the ward, but she wasn't there. He checked his watch, and found it was after five. He wondered where she was. Had she gone off duty? Possibly. Another team was on take, and there was no reason why she should still be in the hospital.

She was probably at home, in that big, solid, safe Victorian house with her parents and her baby.

Lucky Annie. He felt an overwhelming wave of loneliness, and with a disgusted sigh he set off for home. He wasn't going to allow himself to wallow in self-pity. He bought the paper on the way, but there were hardly any properties in it. Apparently Thursday was property day, so he would have to wait until then. He went on the Internet instead, trawling through the property agents and looking for things in the area, but they seemed to give frustratingly few details.

He gave up, and went into the kitchen to make himself a cup of coffee. More coffee. Oh, damn.

He opened a bottle of wine instead, threw an instant meal into the microwave and was just glad his mother wasn't watching him. Alcohol and cholesterol. Brilliant combination. It was a good job he'd spent all that time training as a doctor.

It was only eight o'clock and still light, so he took

himself off for a walk. The park was still open, and he went into it, exploring all the many intersecting paths. He found a slide, set into the hill, and the duck pond, and a children's playground with bark chippings and rope bridges and brightly coloured ducks on springs. There were slides and swings and a big wooden frame like a mini adventure playground, and he wondered how long it would be before Annie's baby was playing in there.

It was deserted now, of course. All the little tiny children would be at home tucked up safely in their beds. He realised it was getting dark, and that the park gates would be locked at dusk. In which case, if he didn't want to risk an undignified scramble over the spiked railings and the possibility of impaling his nether regions, he'd better leave.

He made his way back to the nearest gate, which by coincidence was almost opposite Annie's house. The lights were on in the kitchen at the front, and he could see her sitting at the table. Her mother—he assumed it was her mother—was busy at the sink, and it looked a curiously homely scene.

The loneliness ate at him again, and dragging his eyes away he strode home. It was too late to attack the garden, and the house didn't belong to him, so knocking the wall down would be a little embarrassing. Pity. He felt like a little demolition.

He'd talk to her in the morning, try and clear the air a little. He'd tell her that he'd seen her getting out of the taxi, and point out that she didn't need to lie to him. He wasn't so thick-skinned that he couldn't take a hint.

Good idea. He picked up the bottle of wine and a glass, and went into the sitting room, searching fruitlessly for something on the television that would hold his attention. Predictably, there was nothing, and the wine certainly wasn't worth staying up for.

Ah, well. He'd have an early night. After his lack of sleep and broken dreams the night before, it probably wouldn't go amiss, and he had a long list in the morning.

That meant he would be operating with Annie again, and at the thought his heart pounded heavily against his ribs.

Idiot.

When was he ever going to learn?

There was no opportunity to talk to Annie the following day. The list was long and complicated, and although they were working together, they were never alone. Because they were on take, they also had emergencies to deal with, including one nasty RTA during the early afternoon which had them both working at full stretch.

They were working side by side on a case, trying desperately to repair a torn aorta before their patient, a teenage girl, bled to death. It was hopeless. It was completely impossible to patch the tear, and although they worked flat out, she arrested three times on the table and in the end they had to admit defeat.

Max hated to lose a patient. He particularly hated to lose so young a patient, with all her future ahead of her. He spoke to her parents while Annie and the nurses tidied her up, and then he was called down to

A and E for another suspected surgical admission. While he was there, Annie was called back again to a child with suspected appendicitis in another cubicle.

'Why are they all picking today?' he growled as he passed her in the corridor.

She gave him a fleeting smile, and his heart lifted. Lord, she was lovely. Just having her around made him feel better.

Frustrated, but better.

Finally, at about six-thirty, he managed to get away from the hospital. Steve was on call now, and barring another critical emergency he was able to relax.

And that, of course, meant he had time to think about Annie. He still hadn't talked to her yet about not trusting him, and he really wanted to before very much longer.

He glanced at his watch. A quarter to seven. The shops would be shut, but there was a supermarket not too far away which had flowers. Checking his mirrors quickly, he spun the wheel and did a U-turn that earned him a blast on the horn from a passing motorist, and once at the supermarket he scanned the endless bouquets lined up in buckets.

There were big ones and small ones, some gaudy, some colour co-ordinated in red and gold or yellows or pinks, some with roses, some with lilies.

What would she like? What kind of person was she?

He walked round the end of the display and then he saw them. White lilies, with dark green foliage and greenish-white spider chrysanths—simple and unfussy. He hesitated for a moment, wondering if they were a bit funereal, but there was nothing else he liked and he wasn't giving her red roses.

Not unless he wanted them rammed down his throat.

Although maybe she'd like them…

He gave up, paid for the flowers and left. He went home, showered and shaved, then with a mental girding of his loins he walked round to her house and rang the doorbell.

It echoed in the long, high hall, and after a moment he heard swift footsteps approaching. The door swung in and he got his first close look at her mother—small, slender, grey-haired but dressed in jeans and a T-shirt liberally splashed with water.

Bathtime for the baby?

'Can I help you?' she asked, her eyes scanning him quickly and settling on the flowers with a flicker of curiosity.

'Yes—my name's Max Williamson. I'm a colleague of Annie's. I wondered if she was in.'

Her mother's eyes flicked back to his face, then widened slightly before she collected herself. 'Um—no, she's not,' she said. 'She's gone shopping. I'm her mother, by the way. My name's Jill. Do come in, she may not be long. Can I get you a coffee?'

Max hesitated, then shook his head. 'No, that's not necessary. I don't want to trouble you,' he assured her, feeling a curious wave of disappointment. 'If you could just give her the flowers?'

He handed them over, and she took them, still looking at him searchingly. 'Are you sure you won't come in? It's no trouble, the kettle's always on and I was just about to sit down with a drink myself.'

He was torn, but he didn't know what, if anything, Annie had told her mother about him and he didn't want to put his foot in it. 'Thank you, it's very kind of you, but I won't stop,' he told her with a slight smile.

She nodded. 'All right.' Her eyes searched his face again. 'Any message?'

'No—no, there's no message.' None that he could give her mother, anyway.

He stepped back and gave her a fleeting smile, then turned and walked away. He didn't hear the door close until he was round the corner, and then he kicked himself. He should have stayed. She might only have been five minutes, and then he could have talked to her, right there in the house with her mother to chaperone so she didn't need to feel nervous.

He almost went back, but the idiocy of it suddenly dawned on him and he carried on, back to his lonely, gloomy little rented house. He felt oddly dispirited. This post, his first consultancy, was supposed to have been a new start, to get him away from memories of his disastrous relationship with Fiona and the futile year he'd spent mourning the loss of Annie.

And now she was here, and his new start was just a continuation of the lonely and frustrating period he'd thought he'd left behind, only magnified tenfold because she was always there, looking wary and distant and right in his personal space.

He couldn't even come home and escape her!

Well, it was still daylight. He changed into his tatty

old clothes, went out into the garden and dug over what had obviously been a vegetable patch.

He had no intention of growing vegetables—in fact, the sooner he could find another house, the better—but the exercise took his mind off Annie and might ensure a decent night's sleep, and it was less likely to get him in trouble than putting his fist through a wall.

He leant on the spade and sighed in disgust. What was it about Annie that brought all his emotions roaring to the surface? He felt like a randy, aggressive teenager. Any minute now he'd get spots, for heaven's sake!

He threw the spade into the shed, shut the door and went back inside. There was still half a bottle of wine left in the fridge. He'd have a glass, watch some television and then go to bed.

Annie slipped her key into the lock, let herself in and found her mother sitting in the kitchen.

'Hi, Mum. I've done a big shop—I didn't really mean to, but I got sort of carried away— Oh, nice flowers. Who are they for?'

'You.'

Annie nearly dropped the bag she was juggling. 'Me?' she squeaked. She put the bag down on the worktop and went over to the sink, staring at them suspiciously.

'Who from?'

'Max.'

She spun round, her hand on her chest. 'Max? But— How? When? How did they get here?'

'He brought them.'

'Himself?'

'Yes, himself. Why?'

She felt the panic rising. 'Because he doesn't know where I live. I went round there on Monday night, and I took a taxi when I left. I said I was going on somewhere else.'

'Why?'

She swallowed. 'Why?' she repeated, stalling for time. Lord, she couldn't tell her mother the truth! 'Well, because…a new colleague and all that. I don't know very much about him—'

'But he is the father of your child.'

Her mother's voice was calm and unemotional, and Annie felt the blood drain from her face. She sat down with a plonk at the table, her mouth working soundlessly. 'How?' she finally said. 'How did you know?'

'I just looked at him. Darling, he's got Alice's eyes—or rather, I suppose, she's got his. It's obvious. They're like peas in a pod.'

'Oh, lord.' Annie scrubbed her hands over her face and sat there, her fingers pressed to her lips, her mind whirling. Then a sudden and unwelcome thought occurred to her. 'Mum, did he see her? Alice? Was she with you?'

Her mother shook her head. 'No, darling. She was in bed, asleep.'

'Thank God for that. Mum, if he comes round again, I don't want him to see her, is that clear? He'll know straight away, and I can't risk her security. I don't know enough about him.'

Jill stood up and went over to the kettle, switching

it on, then started to potter with the shopping. 'Is this for you or me?' she asked, taking out a packet of pasta.

Annie looked at her blankly. She couldn't concentrate on pasta. She was torn between panic because Max knew where she lived and might therefore see Alice and realise the truth before she was ready to tell him, and delight that he'd brought her such beautiful flowers. She absolutely loved lilies, and the arrangement was precisely what she would have chosen for herself. How had he known that?

'I don't suppose,' her mother said mildly, 'that you'd like to explain?'

Annie groaned and dropped her head onto her folded arms. 'Not really,' she said. 'I'm not sure I can.'

'I take it you worked together, before Peter—well, before he was ill.'

She shook her head. 'No. I met him in the Lake District—he was there with his fiancée when Peter and I went up last May. It sounds awful, because I knew next to nothing about him, but we just—'

'Clicked?' her mother offered.

Annie nodded. 'Absolutely. I've never felt like that with anyone. He was wonderful to be with, brilliant company but not demanding—just wonderful. We went up Helvellyn—it was when Peter had hurt his foot and Fiona was refusing to go for another walk, so we'd gone together. Then when we got back they weren't there, so we asked the hotel to fix us a picnic and we took their little boat out on the lake, and there was a cove, and—well, I don't know how or why, but it just happened.'

Jill sat down again in her chair and slid a mug across the table towards her. 'I can understand that. I felt the same about your father—but, of course, we weren't married to anybody else, so it didn't matter.'

Annie buried her nose in the mug and sighed unsteadily. 'I feel dreadful about Peter, but he never knew. He didn't even know I was pregnant, and at least his parents were already dead and don't think she's their granddaughter, so I don't have to feel guilty about that, but nevertheless—you know how I feel about infidelity!'

She felt tears prickle her eyes and scrubbed them away angrily. Another thought occurred to her. 'Does Dad know?' she asked, dreading the reply.

'Not yet,' her mother told her. 'I thought I'd discuss it with you first, hear your explanation, before I mentioned it to him. You realise he won't be impressed?'

Annie laughed bitterly. 'Just so long as he doesn't hold a gun to Max's head! And anyway, he won't be any less impressed with me than I am with myself, believe me. The only good thing to come out of it is Alice, and for that reason I can't regret it, but there's no way I can just let him back into my life and pick up where we left off!'

'Is he married now?'

She shook her head. 'No. He broke off the engagement straight away.'

'So he's free, and you're free—what's the problem?'

Annie stared at her. 'Mum, it was just physical!'

'Was it? He seemed awfully nice to me. Don't you think it would be an idea to give it a chance?

Assuming, of course, that you don't find him wildly unattractive now?'

'Not a chance,' she muttered under her breath.

'Well, then,' her mother said with satisfaction. 'Why don't you go round there now and thank him for the flowers? After all, he is Alice's father, whether he knows it or not, and you really ought to tell him. It would give you a chance to get to know him better.'

It all made perfect sense, of course, but she could feel panic rising in her throat as she walked round there. The light was on in the sitting room, and she rang the doorbell and stood waiting, her hands rammed into her pockets to stop her wringing them.

A shadow fell across the glass panel at the top, and the door swung inwards.

'Annie.'

She swallowed and dredged up a smile. 'I came to thank you for the flowers,' she began, and he opened the door further and drew her in.

'You don't have to thank me. It was just a way of getting to talk to you, but you were out. Come in. I was having a glass of wine—I'm sorry about the clothes, I've been digging the garden.'

She glanced down and noticed the worn jeans and tatty T-shirt, and suppressed a smile. He looked good in them. Oh, darn it, she wasn't supposed to be thinking things like that! Concentrate, Annie, she chided herself.

She followed him down the hall to the kitchen, and he poured her a glass of chilled white wine and handed it to her. 'Here—it's nothing special, just a dry

Muscat. Are you hungry? I've got a few snacky things, or I can cook.'

Her stomach rumbled, and she realised she hadn't eaten. 'Actually, I'm starving,' she confessed.

'Beans on toast? It's quick and easy and I have the ingredients, which is always a plus.'

She smiled. 'Sounds wonderful. Thanks. Can I do anything?'

He chuckled. 'I think I can manage beans on toast. You just prop up the worktop and talk to me while I cook. There's a stool under there.'

So she hooked out the bar stool and perched on it and watched him as he put the bread in the toaster and opened the beans and tipped them out into a pan. It was a joy to watch him. His muscles rippled as he moved, and his movements were fluid and supple.

She remembered she was being wary of him, and still didn't know how he'd found out her address. She couldn't let herself get distracted.

'Just as a matter of interest,' she said cautiously, 'how did you know where I lived?'

He gave the beans a stir, lowered the heat and turned to face her, his expression carefully blank. 'I went for a walk on Monday night, after you'd left,' he said. 'I saw you getting out of the taxi.'

'Ah.' Oh, damn. She'd never thought of that.

'Yes, ah,' he echoed. 'Care to explain?'

'I had a call from my friend while I was in the taxi,' she lied frantically. 'She couldn't make it.'

His brow arched slightly in disbelief. 'Is that right?'

Annie sighed and gave in. 'No,' she admitted. 'I just didn't want you to know where I lived. I was still in shock. I didn't think I'd ever see you again. To find you were my new boss—well, it was a bit much to take in. I needed a bit of space—time to think things through, come to terms with it.'

He nodded. 'I wondered if that was it. You could have just said so, you know,' he added mildly. 'I'm quite amenable to suggestion, and I will respect your wishes about this relationship, even if they run contra to mine.'

She sighed again. 'I don't know what my wishes are,' she told him honestly. 'I feel confused and stupidly nervous.'

Max laughed a little grimly. 'I don't think it's stupid to feel nervous. What we had was a one-off. We have no idea where it might have taken us, given a chance.' He turned back to the beans, stirring them again and switching the heat off before buttering the toast and pouring the beans on top.

'Here.' He gave her one of the plates, scooped up a handful of cutlery from a drawer and headed towards the sitting room. She followed him, plate in one hand, glass in the other, and perched on the comfy chair to eat, wondering all the while if he'd dropped the subject.

Apparently not. 'It is a bit odd, though, I'll give you that,' he went on in a matter-of-fact tone, fork poised in the air. 'Here we are, total strangers, and yet we shared what for me anyway was the most incredible experience of my life. I'm almost afraid that reality will tarnish the memory, but so far I have to say it's done quite the opposite.'

Annie nearly choked on her beans. His tone was so casual, he could have been talking about the weather!

And then she looked up and met his eyes and saw the slow burn of desire in them, and realised he was being far from casual. She looked hastily away, hot colour flooding her cheeks, and carefully—much too carefully—cut her toast into tiny pieces.

'Annie? It's OK. I'm just telling you so you know I'm still interested. It's not meant to be a threat.'

She looked up at him again, and he smiled, a gentle, encouraging smile that calmed her. She returned it a little unsteadily. 'Thanks.'

'My pleasure. Eat up.'

She did. She realised she'd hardly eaten anything since she'd seen him again on Monday morning, and she was ravenous. In no time at all her plate was scraped clean, and he was sitting back in his corner of the sofa with an indulgent smile on his face.

'What?' she said, torn between laughter and defensiveness.

'You look as if you needed that. Still hungry? I can make more toast. I've probably got an instant frozen something in the freezer if you're really starving.'

'Toast would be nice,' she admitted, and he stood up with a fluid, easy movement and went into the kitchen, leaving her alone for a moment to gather her thoughts.

So he was still interested. And so, judging by the thudding of her heart and the joy she could feel simmering in her veins, was she.

Oh, yipes.

He came back into the room and perched on the

arm of her chair, resting a hand on her shoulder. 'It's good to see you again, Annie,' he said quietly. 'I really thought we'd never meet again, and now we have, maybe we'll get a proper chance at this relationship.'

'I don't want to rush it,' she told him with the last vestige of her feeble restraint. Just his presence so close to her was undermining her resolve at the speed of light. She just hoped he had more self-control than she did.

'Nor do I,' he agreed. 'We'll take it steady, one step at a time.'

He stood up again and went back to the kitchen, returning with a tray of coffee and a heap of hot buttered toast. 'There—tuck in.'

It was gorgeous. Horribly fattening, but it wouldn't hurt her to put back on some of the weight she'd lost. She was skin and bone these days, she realised, despite her mother's attempts to feed her up. Maybe Max and his hot buttered toast were just what she needed.

He put on some music, something soft and lazy and romantic, and gradually she relaxed. She slipped off her shoes and curled her feet under her bottom, wrapped her hands round her mug of coffee and laughed at all his silly jokes.

He was laughing at hers, too, and she suddenly realised she hadn't felt so happy or so relaxed for ages, not since—heavens. Not since the last time they'd been together, when they'd walked up Helvellyn and sat looking out over the sea in the distance and talked about nothing.

'I ought to go home,' she said, glancing at her watch. 'My mother's babysitting.' Not, she had to admit, that her mother would mind if she was late, but the cosiness was getting dangerous.

Max stood up and pulled her gently to her feet, easing her into his arms. His head rested beside hers, and she could feel his heart beating. Her arms slid round him of their own volition, and he sighed softly and nuzzled his face into her hair.

'You're beautiful, Annie,' he murmured.

'That won't get you anywhere,' she protested laughingly, but he didn't laugh back.

'I'm not trying to get anywhere. I'm just telling you the truth.'

Warmth flooded her—warmth and need. She eased away.

'I really do have to go home.'

'I'll walk you,' he said, in a voice that brooked no argument.

It only took three minutes, and as they reached the door, it opened and her father stood there.

'Annie, darling, you're back.'

She glared at him, but he ignored her and held his hand out, giving Max a grim and dangerous smile. 'Geoff Turner—Annie's father.'

Max shook his hand. 'Max Williamson. It's good to meet you, sir.'

'Come in, come in,' he said, eyeing Max up and down like an old lion checking out a potential interloper into the pride. Oh, hell.

'Thank you,' Max said, stepping over the threshold into the hall, apparently unaware of his fate. How could he be so blind?

Her father studied him openly. 'You look awfully

young to be a consultant,' he said, and Max gave a wry laugh.

'I'm thirty-two,' he said. 'I must just be wearing well.'

'Things are different these days, of course. I wasn't a consultant until I was thirty-eight. Fancy a night-cap?'

Annie nearly had a fit. 'He can't,' she said desperately. 'He's operating in the morning.'

Max turned to her, one eyebrow raised slightly. 'I am?' he murmured, knowing full well he wasn't.

'Yes,' she said firmly.

He shrugged and smiled at her father. 'She knows the schedule better than me—I'm still finding my feet. And, of course, she's right, if I am operating then I'll have an early start, so I'd better call it a day.'

And then, just when she thought everything was going to be all right, he turned to her, bent his head and brushed his lips lightly over her mouth.

'Goodnight, Annie. I'll see you tomorrow,' he murmured, then with a wave of his hand to her father, he went out into the night, leaving her rooted to the floor.

'He seems a nice enough chap,' her father said, looking at her for the first time as he shut the door. 'More your sort than Peter. Not that I wish to speak ill of the dead, but I never could see what you saw in him. Cold fish. I like Max.'

He dropped a kiss on her forehead and patted her shoulder.

'We all make mistakes,' he said. 'He looks like one of your better ones.'

And with that he flicked off the outside light, locked

the door and put the chain across, and headed off up the stairs to bed, leaving Annie standing in the hall like a stunned mullet.

Her father approved of Max?

Wonders would never cease!

CHAPTER FIVE

'So I have a list this morning, do I?'

'Don't make me jump!' Annie exclaimed, clapping a hand over her chest and spinning round, a laugh on her lips.

'You lied to your father,' Max said, *sotto voce.*

'I had to get you away from him. He was getting...'

'Paternal?'

His mouth kicked up into the crooked, teasing smile that she loved.

'He gives every man that comes to the house the third degree. He thinks I'm still a teenager. I just thought I'd save you the embarrassment.'

Max grinned. 'I think I can handle your father,' he murmured. 'Fancy a coffee?'

'I'd love a coffee,' Anne assured him, 'but I don't think I've got time. I've got to check up on yesterday's patients.'

'I'll give you a hand with them,' he suggested, 'and then I can steal you away with a clean conscience.'

'Don't you have something you ought to be doing, or a clinic or something?'

'No, it's my admin morning and I've done it all because I'm a good boy and efficient and organised, so now I'm free to play.'

She stifled her smile. He might be free to play, but she wasn't, not really. Still, if he helped her then she could probably squeeze a few minutes. 'OK, if you insist.'

'I insist,' he insisted with a smile. 'Now, who do you want me to look at?'

She handed him a wadge of notes. 'Try this lot.'

She turned away, trying to hide her grin, and bumped straight into Damien. He was giving her an odd look, but she wasn't going to stand there and explain herself to him. She hurried away, notes in hand, to her first patient. As she reached his bedside, she looked over her shoulder and saw Max and Damien staring after her. Max winked, a slow, lazy wink that went straight to her knees. How she concentrated through her examination of her patients she didn't know, but finally she had finished and she returned the notes to the nursing station to find Max there, still chatting to Damien.

'Haven't you started yet?' she asked him, and he just tutted gently.

'Such a lack of respect,' he murmured, and Damien's eyebrows shot up into his hairline. Max ignored him and tapped her on the nose. 'Actually, cheeky chops, I've finished, so how about that coffee?'

'Sounds good to me,' she said. 'I might find time to cram in a cake as well. I didn't get round to breakfast this morning, Alice was fussing. I think she might be getting another tooth.'

'When am I going to get to get to see this baby of yours?' he asked, and she felt a jolt of shock. This was a problem she hadn't anticipated, although she should have done, if she'd had any sense it all. She might have known that Max would want to be involved in every moment of her life.

'I'm not sure it's a very good idea for you to see her,' she said with deliberate calm. 'Not yet, at any rate. I don't want her getting emotionally attached to you and then getting upset if things go wrong.'

He paused at the coffee-machine in the canteen and looked at Annie searchingly. 'OK,' he said quietly. 'It was just an idea. I'm not trying to crowd you or elbow my way in where I'm not wanted.'

Oh, rats. Now she'd hurt his feelings and she really hadn't meant to. She stuck a cup under the spout and pressed the cappuccino button. The cup filled with frothy coffee, and she sprinkled the top liberally with chocolate powder and plonked it on the tray. 'I didn't mean to imply you're trying to elbow your way in,' she said carefully. 'I'm just trying to protect her.'

He put a cup of black coffee down beside her frothy concoction and shot her a crooked grin.

'I know,' he said gently. 'I do understand. It must be very difficult, being a single parent. You've had a hell of a lot to deal with in the last year and a bit, and the last thing I want to do is add to it. Now, how about that cake?'

She picked up a really gooey apricot Danish and stuck it on a plate, and he pulled a face and picked up a chocolate muffin.

She laughed. 'And that's better?' she said.

'Less gloopy. Anyway, I like chocolate. Is there a law against it?'

She held up her hands in surrender. 'Absolutely not.

Each to his own. Come on, we can't hang about here all day, I've got lots to do.'

'I expect your boss is a real slave-driver,' he said with a grin. 'We'd better not upset him.'

They went into the coffee-lounge and sat down on a low, comfy sofa in the corner. He didn't seem to be in the least bit worried about being seen with her, and when she dropped a sticky dollop of Danish down her chin, he didn't have the slightest hesitation in wiping it off with her napkin in a frankly proprietorial gesture that left her slightly flustered.

'I told you it was too gloopy,' he said with a smile, and she forgot about everybody else in the room. It was as if the sun had come out, and suddenly she didn't care what anybody else thought of them. It was nobody's business but their own, and if he wasn't worried, she wasn't.

Predictably her bleeper distracted her, and she had to leave him and go to A and E. As she went down the corridor Mike Taylor, one of the SHOs, fell into step beside her.

'That looked cosy,' he said casually. 'Trying to sleep your way to the top?'

She stopped in her tracks and glared at him. 'How *dare* you make such a disgusting suggestion?' she snapped.

He threw up his hands in surrender. 'Don't shout at me, lady. If I looked like you, I'd probably try it.'

'You are vile,' she muttered, turning away and hurrying towards A and E. She heard footsteps following her, and spun round, saying, 'Leave me alone!' only to find Max standing there, looking startled.

'Annie?' he said questioningly, and she closed her eyes and sighed.

'Sorry. I thought it was someone else.'

'Mike. I saw you talking to him—you didn't look impressed. That's why I followed you. What did he say?'

'He accused me of sleeping my way to the top,' she snapped, shouldering a door out of the way.

'I wish,' Max muttered, catching the door as it swung back in his face. 'I take it you put him straight?'

'I tried.' She stopped and pulled out her ponytail band, scraped her hair back and replaced the band almost viciously. 'Look, I'm going to be late. I have to go. Just—maybe it would be a good idea if we weren't seen together like that in the hospital.'

'Like what? Friends?'

She shrugged. 'Whatever. I have to go. Thanks for the coffee.'

He winked at her, and she turned and almost ran the last few steps to A and E. Maybe if she buried herself in work she'd forget about Mike and his vile suggestion...

Max went up to his office and asked the switchboard to page Mike Taylor. Moments later the phone rang.

'Yes, sir?'

'I'm in my office. Get up here now.'

'I'm a bit busy—'

'Tough. If it isn't life or death, be here. That's an order.' He banged the phone back on the hook and glared at it. How dare he insult Annie like that?

In the two minutes it took Mike to get to his office, Max had calmed down. Not much, just enough that he didn't put his fist straight down Mike's throat as he walked through the door.

The man strolled in and hitched up a chair, and Max gave him a chilling look. 'Did I invite you to sit down?'

Mike stood up again, suddenly seeming to notice just how angry Max was. He paled a little. 'What can I do for you, sir?' he said.

'You can apologise to Dr Shaw, for one,' he said, his voice clipped. 'How dare you say anything like that to her? You were totally out of order.'

'I'm sorry.'

'I should damn well hope so, but you can tell her that yourself. Not that it's any of your blasted business, but we happen to be old friends, and if we want to have coffee together, pardon me for pointing it out but I don't believe we need your permission. The other thing you can do for me is keep firmly out of my way and my registrar's way, and when you have to speak to either of us, we'll have the professional respect and courtesy we're entitled to.'

He turned away. 'That's all. And watch it. Anything else like this and you'll be finding yourself another job.'

The door closed with a muted click, and he leant his head against the window and stared down into the car park below. Falling out with his SHO on his fourth day in the hospital was hardly to be recommended, but he'd never liked the man from the moment he'd met him.

He was cocky and opinionated, and destined one day to make one of those arrogant consultants that put the patients' backs up and alienated the general public. Well, not if Max had anything to say about it. He'd have to prove himself first before he'd give him a reference worth having, and just at the moment that was going to be an uphill struggle!

Oh, hell, what did it matter? He was a junior doctor, and with any luck not so far gone that Max slicing him down to size wouldn't make a lasting impression. If it didn't work—well, frankly Max would happily have another go.

He smacked a fist into his open palm and ground his teeth, then dropped into his chair and swivelled it, propping his feet on the desk. Maybe Annie was right and they shouldn't see so much of each other in public. He didn't care if people talked about him, but he cared for Annie, and if they were saying things like that—

His bleeper squawked, and he picked up the phone and called the switchboard.

'Oh, Mr Williamson, you're wanted on the ward. Dr Shaw would like to see you.'

'Thanks.'

He hung up, shrugged into his white coat, picked up his bleeper and headed for the lift.

Annie was flummoxed. A patient who had come in for elective surgery on her gall bladder was complaining of constant excruciating pain in her abdomen, which didn't fit with her gallstones.

The pain was just wrong somehow, too severe and

in the wrong place, and her abdomen was rigid. It looked for all the world like peritonitis, but she couldn't imagine why.

She was hugely relieved to see Max striding down the ward towards her, his long legs eating up the ground.

'What's the problem?' he said, quickly scanning the woman with his eyes.

'Abdominal pain of sudden onset, rigid abdomen—she's in for cholecystectomy tomorrow.'

He frowned, peeled back the bedclothes and very, very gently touched her abdomen.

The woman let out a scream of pain, and he straightened, his lips pursed.

'OK, let's get some painkiller into her. Has she had anything yet?'

Annie shook her head. 'I wanted to get you first. If you'd been held up, I would have given her something, but it seems an odd pain for gallstones.'

'It's nothing to do with gallstones. I'll lay odds she's got a perforation somewhere from taking anti-inflammatories for the pain. Let's get her comfortable and then she needs a trip to Theatre because, whatever's wrong, it's urgent and surgical.'

He wrote her up for diamorphine, injected it slowly into her arm and watched as she gradually relaxed a fraction and began to cry silent tears of relief.

'Don't worry, Mrs Bradley, we'll sort you out,' he reassured her. He turned to Annie. 'Do we have next of kin we can contact?'

'Yes—Damien's doing it. He thought she might not

be up to signing a consent form and he suspected you'd want to operate.'

He nodded. 'Right, let's get her up to Theatre. I'm not going to worry about consent forms, we've got one already for the op tomorrow and we need to move fast. She's getting shocky. I want a line in and normal saline, please, and cross-match for transfusion if necessary.'

He rattled off a whole list of other tests that needed doing, and Damien jotted them down, then inserted the giving set and withdrew enough blood for the tests before setting up the saline drip.

'Right, we'll go and scrub, if you could send her up, Damien, please?'

The charge nurse nodded, and Max and Annie headed for the door.

'I think you can do this one,' he said to her as they went out into the corridor. 'Should be nice and obvious what it is.'

'I hope so,' Annie muttered, wondering what she knew about perforations.

'Don't worry,' he said, throwing her a grin. 'I'll be there. I won't let you mess it up or forget anything.'

He was right. It was nice and obvious, a huge perforation in the patient's stomach, and because Max was there, watching, she felt she could relax and do what she thought was appropriate.

Occasionally he made a comment, such as 'Take a little more—that's better' or 'Try a different angle', but most of the time he just held the retractors and watched in silence. And when she'd finished, he grinned at her, his eyes crinkling over the mask, and said, 'Well done.' She felt like a million dollars.

She'd done the gall bladder as well—there was no point in putting the woman through two operations, and the gall bladder had been pretty critical on its own—so by the time she'd finished Annie felt quietly pleased with herself.

'I'm not convinced you needed me at all for that,' Max said with a smile as they left the theatre.

'Oh, I don't know. You were quite useful, holding the retractors, and you're very decorative,' she replied with a twinkle in her eye, and he chuckled.

'Such a lack of respect— Oh, talking of which, have you seen Mike Taylor yet?'

She felt her smile fade. 'No—why?'

'Just curious.'

She frowned at him. 'Have you said something?'

'Just a quiet word in his ear.'

Somehow she didn't believe that. She couldn't imagine it would have been 'just' anything, although it might have been quiet. Deathly quiet, she imagined. Max wasn't the sort to shout at colleagues or underlings. Oh, dear. She wondered what Mike would say when he saw her next, and decided she didn't really care. So long as Max wasn't affected by it, she could live with the rumours. She knew the truth—and it was infinitely worse than Mike had suggested.

Max left the hospital shortly after Mrs Bradley came back down from Recovery, and when Annie got home it was to find a note for her that had been pushed through the letterbox.

'Are you busy? Still don't know your phone number, but I'm going to look at a house at seven. Fancy coming? Ring me.'

He'd written down his phone number, and she looked at her watch and bit her lip. Seven was a little early. She wanted to bath Alice and put her to bed, and just recently she'd been a little unsettled.

She rang Max on the cordless phone while Alice was sitting up splashing in the bath, and nearly dropped the phone in the water.

'I can't talk, I'm bathing the baby. I just wanted to say I might come—what time are you leaving?'

'Seven. The appointment's not till half past, but I'm not sure of the way. Why, what's the problem? I can probably change the time.'

'No, don't worry,' she said. 'I just don't want to leave before Alice is asleep. She's been restless and unsettled recently, and I think she's teething. And she's about to fall over. I'll ring you,' she said hurriedly, and dropped the phone to the floor just in time to catch Alice as she toppled backwards with a giggle.

'You're a monster,' she told her little daughter, and scooped her out of the bath, snuggling her up in the fluffy towel and cuddling her close. She was damp and sweet-smelling, and Annie ached with the continual pain of parting from her daily. She wanted to be with her, to see her take her first step, say her first word, do her first wee on the potty.

Swallowing hard, she dashed away the tears against her shoulders and hugged Alice. Predictably her daughter cried out and wriggled to be free, and Annie patted her dry and dressed her in her nightclothes.

She was settled in her cot by five to seven, but

Annie hadn't changed or eaten or even so much as run a brush through her hair. She looked at herself in the mirror in despair.

Her top was soaked, she was covered in baby powder and her hair needed washing—and the doorbell was ringing. Please, she prayed, don't let it be Max. But, of course, it was.

Annie stuck her head out of the flat door and pulled a face at him. 'I'm a mess. I can't possibly go like this, and I don't want to make you late.'

He walked calmly down the hall, scanned her spattered form with laughing eyes and suppressed a smile. 'Bathtime?' he murmured, and she rolled her eyes.

'You noticed.'

'Drag on some jeans and a clean T-shirt or something. It's only the estate agent, it's an executor's sale.'

'I haven't even eaten.'

'Nor have I. We'll get something afterwards.'

She gave up, because he clearly wasn't going to, and anyway she wanted to see the house, because at some point she knew Alice would end up spending time with him in his home, and if for no other reason, she wanted to see it.

And it's nothing to do with seeing if you'd like to live in it yourself, of course, she mocked herself silently as she dressed. Ever the optimist.

She stuffed her feet into her comfy old loafers, grabbed her bag, stuck her head round Alice's door and checked that she'd gone off and then ran.

Her mother cut off her list of instructions.

'I can deal with Alice. I don't need to ring your mobile. You go and have a good time.'

'We're just looking at a house,' she protested, but her mother smiled one of those smiles and ushered them out.

Oh, hell. Drat her parents, they were both besotted with Max.

His car was outside, a three-year-old Audi estate, nothing flashy but very respectable. It was also quite quick, she discovered moments later as he flipped out onto the main road and headed north-east.

'So what are we going to look at?' she asked.

'A 1930s house on the edge of town. It's been lived in by the same owner from new, and according to the agent it probably hasn't been decorated since it was built. It needs rewiring, plumbing, new bathroom and heating, kitchen—you name it—but it's in half an acre, it's got four bedrooms and I can afford it, which I'd never do if it was already done up.'

It sounded lovely, but Annie was good at painting mental pictures and the reality seldom lived up to them.

He passed her a piece of paper with the address on it, and a map with a red splodge marking the house's approximate whereabouts. 'Can you get us there?'

'Easy,' she said, finding one of the elements of her mental picture had been right, at least. She'd chosen the right area. It only took them ten minutes to get there, so they were in plenty of time even though she'd stopped to change and tidy herself up.

They cruised slowly down the road, looking for the elusive numbers that were tucked away on gateposts hidden by laurel hedges, or on doors, or beside doors—it was as if everyone wanted their address to be a secret, she thought.

'No wonder the emergency services complain so bitterly about finding addresses,' Max said, and then suddenly they saw it.

Big and solid and built of red brick, it stood at a slight angle to the road, with an arched entrance to the open porch in the centre, a large bay window to one side, a flat window to the other. It was slightly L-shaped at the front, with an interesting roof-line, and although there was only a small wooden garage at one side there was room for a proper brick-built double garage in its place.

Max pulled up on the road outside and they got out, walking slowly up the overgrown drive.

'The back garden should be west facing,' Annie said, remembering the map, and she looked up to see the position of the sun. It was behind the house, and would now be flooding the garden with evening light and showing it in all its tangled glory.

Max nodded thoughtfully. 'If it's as good as the front garden, it's going to take a bit of work to rescue it. It can't have been touched for years, but there are some roses over there sticking up out of the jungle with beautiful blooms on them, and there are all sorts of other things. I don't know what they are.'

Annie looked and reeled off a list. 'Day-lilies, perennial geraniums, dianthus, lavender—and given a little care and attention, it'll be beautiful. That's a hydrangea,' she said, pointing to a huge plant in the middle of the overgrown drive, smothered in heavy mops of pink, 'and I know the lawn around the edges is knee-high and unkempt, but it's easy to imagine it tidied up. Oh, Max, it's going to be gorgeous!'

Max wished he could see it through her eyes. She was sparkling with enthusiasm, and as he knew next to nothing about gardening, he would have to believe her when she said it could be rescued.

'It is lovely,' he said slowly. 'The house looks a good size, too, and the roof looks OK. No obvious cracks in the walls.'

He scanned the window-frames, and although some of them were peeling, the wood seemed solid enough. He poked one with his car keys, and it was firm. Good. With everything else to do, he really didn't need to replace all the windows as well.

He heard a car pull up behind him, and turned to see the estate agent approaching, one hand clutching a few sheets of paper, the other one outstretched towards him.

'Mr Williamson!' the man said. 'I'm from the agents. You have a set of details?'

'No, I don't. I only saw the property in the paper this afternoon.'

'Take these, then, it'll help you remember afterwards.' He handed the papers over, shook hands with Annie and said, 'Nice to meet you, Mrs Williamson.'

Max didn't bother to correct him. He was too busy thinking it actually sounded rather good, and anyway, it was irrelevant.

The agent unlocked the door and pushed it open, sweeping all the junk mail out of the way with his foot. 'It's a while since we came here—we had a buyer but he dropped out and so it's back on the market again. Why don't I leave you to have a look round on your own? I'll be around if you need me.'

Max nodded and opening the details he went first into the large room with the bay window. It was obviously meant to be the dining-room, and overlooked the front garden. He could imagine that it would be a lovely place for a lazy breakfast at the weekend, and it had perfect proportions.

On the other side of the hall beside a tiny cloakroom was a room that would make an ideal study, and behind it was a big sitting room facing down the tangled garden. Beside the sitting room was the kitchen, and beyond it a whole collection of odd little rooms and cubby holes that could easily be opened up to make a lovely big kitchen-breakfast room.

He felt excitement building inside him and turned to Annie.

'What do you think?' he asked.

'It could be gorgeous,' she said, and she sounded a little wistful. Suddenly, he felt guilty. She must have had a house with Peter, and now she was living in a little flat at the back of her parents' house, and struggling to bring up her child alone. He wondered about life insurance and whether Peter had had any, or if he had left Annie in debt and with financial difficulties.

Surely not. Peter simply wouldn't have been that disorganised.

'Come on,' he said to Annie, 'let's go upstairs.'

Max led her up the broad, solid oak staircase to the landing, and there they found four good-sized bedrooms, a little dressing-room and a bathroom that was straight out of a museum.

'I'd almost be tempted to keep this as it is,' he said thoughtfully.

'They sell suites just like this now,' Anne replied.

'That tiny dressing-room off the main bedroom would make a perfect *en suite* bathroom,' he added. He tried to picture it, and as he did so he got a startlingly clear image of Annie stepping naked out of the shower tray, hair dripping, water streaming down her body. He groaned inwardly and walked round the bedrooms again, partly to have another look and partly to get a little distance between him and her before he did something stupid.

He could almost hear the echoes of the family that had been brought up here, the thunder of children's feet running up the stairs, the laughter and tears. The late owner must have been one of those children, and the house seemed full of the warmth of happy memories.

As if she'd read his mind, Annie said, 'It's got a lovely atmosphere, hasn't it?'

He looked at her, at the wistful expression on her face, and wondered if there was any hope that she and her baby would be living here with him in the future. The house was crying out for another family, not just Annie and her baby but more children, maybe a boy and another girl, and perhaps a dog in front of the fire and a cat curled up dozing in the sun on the windowsill.

He was getting ahead of himself, building castles in the air, pipe dreams. It wouldn't do to allow himself to get too involved in that particular fantasy. There was still an awfully long way to go before he could be that sure of her, if it ever happened.

He might yet end up here with nothing to keep him warm but the memory of that one stolen moment, he thought, and felt a wave of desolation sweep over him.

He wouldn't give up, though. He was no quitter, and Annie was more important to him than anyone or anything had ever been. All he had to do was convince her…

CHAPTER SIX

THEY found a nice little pub nearby for supper, and while they ate, Max talked enthusiastically about the house. He'd spoken to the agent before they'd left, and had put in an offer which the agent would submit to the executors in the morning. Until they had replied, there was no certainty that the offer would be accepted, and Annie was worried that Max was jumping the gun a little.

Still, she couldn't dampen his enthusiasm. His eyes were alight, and it was interesting to hear him expanding his plans for it. He asked for her opinion on his suggestions, and she was only a little surprised to find how often their views coincided.

'And the garden,' he went on. 'Isn't it amazing? I mean, I know it's a mess, but it's huge and the basic framework's there, and those old trees—I love trees. There were even the remains of an old rope swing on one of them that reminded me of my childhood.'

Annie had noticed—noticed and pictured Alice, and maybe her little brother or sister, playing happily on the swing in the dappled sunshine, while she and Max sat on the flagstone terrace behind the house and watched them indulgently.

And now who was jumping the gun?

Finally, though, even Max ran out of steam and he gave her a rueful grin.

'Sorry, Annie, I'm getting a bit ahead of myself, aren't I?'

She shrugged, twinged with guilt. 'At least you know that you really want it,' she said. 'If you didn't have any ideas, it would be because it hadn't inspired you and so it would be a mistake to buy it, but I think you ought to wait until you know, so it's not so awful if you don't get it.'

He chuckled. 'You're always so sensible, aren't you?' he teased.

She almost laughed aloud. Her, sensible? Not always. Not with him. Now, maybe, but not then. And she found a little bit of her yearning for that irresponsible girl who had given herself so freely and so wholeheartedly to a man she hadn't known and yet instinctively had loved.

But she had Alice now and, however much she might want to throw caution to the winds, she had no choice but to be responsible. There would be no more Alices, no more stolen moments, no more impromptu forays into uncharted territory. She glanced at her watch and pulled a face.

'I really ought to be getting home,' she told him. 'I've used up an awful lot of credit this week with my mother, and I really need to save it for the times that I'm on duty.'

'Do you ever get a babysitter?' he asked her. 'I mean, like a schoolgirl neighbour or someone, instead of your mother?'

She shook her head. 'She'd be woefully offended if I did that, and that's one of the problems, of course. She'd complain if I got anybody else, but it just means

I feel constrained and hardly ever go out—not that I want to go out that often,' she added with a hollow laugh that sounded horribly self-pitying.

Max shot her a crooked grin and got to his feet. 'Come on, then, Cinderella, let's get you back before the chariot turns into a pumpkin.'

Cinderella? Was that how he saw her? Covered in soot, with her fingers worked to the bone and nowhere to go? Oh, lord, if it weren't so close to the truth it would be funny. She groped for her bag under the chair and stood up, and Max ushered her out of the pub and back to his car.

He unlocked the car with the remote-control key, opened the passenger door and waited while she got in, handing her the buckle of the seat belt before he went round to the other side. It was only a simple gesture of courtesy, but it was one he used every time and she found it rather touching.

It was so automatic, so much a part of him that he didn't even think about it. It made her feel curiously cherished, something that was sadly lacking in her life at the moment, and she desperately wished she could forget about circumspection and responsibility and just let matters take their course with him. It wasn't just about sex, it was about having a close physical relationship with someone who cared.

It just seemed such a long time since anybody had *hugged* her, just a simple, honest-to-goodness hug. Apart from her mother, of course, who did it all the time. It wasn't the same, though, and she really missed the feel of a man's arms around her.

No, not a man's arms, Max's arms, she admitted with painful honesty. She never missed Peter's arms.

They were back at her house in ten minutes, and he pulled up outside on the drive, cut the engine and turned to look at her.

'I don't suppose there's any danger of you inviting me in for coffee, is there?' he suggested.

She was horribly tempted. It was only early. There was absolutely no reason why he couldn't come in, and after all they would hardly be alone. Her parents were in the house, and there was always Alice.

And that, of course, was the reason why he couldn't come in, because if Alice woke she would have to get her up, and then he would see her, and then he would know.

She couldn't risk it. With a sigh of regret, she shook her head. 'I'm sorry, Max, but I've got loads to do—washing and ironing, and I really need a shower before I can go to bed.'

It was all absolutely true, but it sounded a really feeble excuse and she thought she saw a brief flicker of disappointment in his eyes. She was about to change her mind and retract her refusal, but he gave her that lovely crooked smile, got out of the car and walked her to the door.

Annie slipped her key into the lock to turn it, but his hand came up and stopped her, and as she looked up he lowered his head and found her mouth with his.

It was a very chaste kiss, really, but her knees threatened to buckle and her heart pounded against her ribs. He started to ease away, but a tiny sound of protest rose in her throat, and with an almost inaudible groan he drew her closer, slanted his mouth over hers and kissed her senseless.

She totally forgot that she was standing on her parents' doorstep, but Max didn't. He grew gentle, easing back until he was raining tiny, tender kisses all over her face. Then he folded her into his arms, tucked her head under his chin and rocked her gently against his heart.

She could feel it pounding, and knew that he felt the chemistry between them just as strongly as she did. He, though, had the strength of mind to pull back. It was a good job that one of them did, she thought shakily, because her brakes had just suffered a comprehensive failure.

'Goodnight, precious,' he murmured. 'Thank you for coming with me to the house. Go and do your washing and your ironing, and think of me.'

He dropped another kiss on her lips, tapped her nose gently with his forefinger and stepped back.

'Sleep well. I'll see you tomorrow.'

She nodded, leaning on the door for support, and watched him drive away with a ridiculous yearning ache in her heart. Seeing him again was opening up all the emotions she'd spent months damping down, and it was becoming increasingly hard to remember just why she was holding him at a distance.

'Alice,' she said a little fiercely. 'Think of Alice.'

But Alice was just like her father, warm and sunny and spontaneous, full of laughter, her eyes even at eight months twinkling with mischief. Thinking of Alice just brought Max to mind, which was a refined form of torture, but there was no way she could regret having had her. She'd been the only decent thing to come out of a truly dreadful year.

However, until she was sure of Max, she didn't dare let him see Alice, because she needed to be absolutely certain he wanted her for the right reasons. Her first marriage had been a hollow sham, and she couldn't bear that to happen to her and Max. She knew enough about him now to know that once he'd found out about his child, he'd insist on doing the decent thing, and Annie couldn't afford to make another mistake, no matter how much she might want to.

One thing she was sensible enough to realise, though. Her relationship with Max might be on the back burner now, but he was slowly and steadily turning up the heat and she wasn't going to have the desire or strength of will to resist him for much longer.

In which case she really needed to visit the clinic at the hospital and make absolutely sure that she and not chance was in charge.

Just in case, of course.

Max was wide awake. All he could think about was the house, and how Annie had seemed to like it, too, and how right 'Mrs Williamson' had sounded on the estate agent's lips.

'You're getting in deep,' he warned himself, but then he gave a sad, humourless little laugh. He'd been in deep since he'd first set eyes on her at the hotel. He didn't believe in destiny, but somehow Annie seemed carved into his future regardless. He couldn't imagine life without her now, but that was probably foolish nonsense and he'd do well to keep his emotions in check.

Hah! Not a likely scenario. He went to bed and dreamed—confused, broken dreams about the house and Annie and a little baby that looked just like him, and when Annie turned round he could see that her body was rounded with pregnancy.

He woke with a start. He'd better not get her pregnant! Not yet, not now. He didn't want them ending up together just because they'd fouled up and were doing 'the right thing'. He'd drop into the sexual health clinic at the hospital tomorrow and make sure he was prepared.

Just in case, of course!

Annie went onto the ward just after eight the next morning, and after she'd spoken to Damien she went straight to Mrs Bradley's bedside and checked her. Mike Taylor had been on in the night and had been called to her a couple of times because of her pain, apparently, and Annie couldn't understand it. Surely Max had written her up for adequate pain relief yesterday?

She had developed raging peritonitis, not unsurprisingly, and the broad-spectrum IV antibiotics she'd been started on the previous afternoon hadn't yet kicked in. Her worst problem, though, and the one which was making her most miserable, was nausea.

'I don't like these painkillers,' she said weakly. 'I need them, but every time I have an injection I just feel sick again, and it only wears off as the pain comes back. Then it starts all over again.'

Annie nodded. She could see from the notes that Mike had written her up for pethidine but had failed to write her up for an anti-emetic to stop her being sick. On top of that her pain relief was wearing off before she had the next dose, which was less than satisfactory. She needed a syringe driver with pain relief and an anti-emetic built in, really, but they didn't have a spare one on the ward—unless Tim Jacobs, their leaking RTA victim, didn't need his any longer.

'Give me a minute. I'll get you something now to stop you feeling sick, and I might be able to find you a much better solution altogether,' she told the distressed woman, and went to find Damien again.

'Mrs Bradley's been really suffering with nausea in the night,' she told him.

'Yes, the agency nurse told me. I'm surprised she noticed. We've had that one before, and I think someone needs to complain about her. She's useless. Most of them are excellent, but to be honest I think she's got a drug problem. I think that's the only reason she does it.'

It was a perennial hazard of their profession, Annie knew, and anyone with a weakness in that direction would find it all too easy to get a steady supply of drugs. Still, she wasn't worried about the agency nurse now, just Mrs Bradley and her pain relief.

'How's Tim Jacobs doing?' she asked Damien.

'Better. Why? Want the syringe driver?'

She grinned. 'You guessed. Can he spare it yet?'

Damien shrugged. 'I would think so. He's much brighter, and he didn't complain in the night. We could have a look if you like, see how much he's used.'

'OK. I don't want him to think we're stealing his pain relief, though.'

'We ought to have enough of them. They're essential bits of kit,' Damien said with a frown. 'We don't usually run short, but we've got a bit of a run on them at the moment. I'm just trying to think if there's anyone else who could spare theirs, but I can't.'

'Let's talk to Tim.'

He was sitting up in bed looking much brighter, and he admitted he hadn't used any pethidine in the night. 'I had a shot before I went to sleep, and the next thing I knew it was morning. Brilliant.'

'So do you need this any more, if we promise not to keep you short of pain relief?'

He shook his head. 'I don't think I do, and to be honest all the tubes and things frighten my wife and daughter, so I'd be quite glad to lose it in a way. It still hurts, but if I can have something else...'

He shrugged, and Annie sighed inwardly with relief. Mrs Bradley could have her pain relief and anti-emetic on demand, and Mr Jacobs's family wouldn't have to be scared by all the kit. Excellent.

Within a few minutes Damien had it set up by Mrs Bradley, delivering an even and measured dose of drugs controlled by her, when she needed them and not when she'd felt bad enough to call and the drugs had finally penetrated her system. This way the drugs were straight into her bloodstream, delivered instantly to the site of the pain, and she would need much less overall than with the other method.

And it wouldn't be up to Mike Taylor to remember to give her anti-emetics if necessary.

Annie checked the notes again, unable to believe that Max hadn't written her up for anything, and there above Mike's scrawl was Max's neat, decisive hand, detailing pethidine and prochlorperazine administration as necessary.

So why had Mike prescribed something else, something less effective, and why hadn't it been noticed? The agency nurse, Annie thought with sudden clarity. Of course—and Mike was too busy nursing his ego to pay attention to trivial detail.

Talking of the devil, he came onto the ward just as she finished checking another patient, and he saw her and looked guilty. Because of Mrs Bradley, or because of what he'd said about sleeping her way to the top?

She didn't care. She was cross with him, and she couldn't be bothered to deal with it tactfully. She walked up to him.

'We need a word,' she said firmly, and wheeled him out of the ward and into the corridor. 'About Mrs Bradley—why did you ignore Mr Williamson's prescription and write her up for pethidine without prochlorperazine?'

His eyes became wary. 'I did?'

'Yes, you did—and anyway, even if he had omitted to prescribe anything for her, didn't it occur to you to give her an anti-emetic with the pain relief?'

'I didn't know she was sick. The night staff didn't call me.'

'That's nonsense,' she snapped. 'You came back

and gave her more later. You must have asked if she'd tolerated it.'

'I thought they'd tell me.'

She rolled her eyes. 'Ask, Dr Taylor. Don't just assume—not anything, not ever, and anticipate. You shouldn't have waited for her to be sick. She's had major abdominal surgery. The last thing she needs is to vomit and rip all her sutures. It's not a case of making her a bit more comfy, it's about not doing damage and maybe saving her life. Whatever, she's got a syringe driver now with pethidine and prochlorperazine, so it's out of your hands, but next time, think!'

He nodded. 'Sorry,' he said, without sounding it in the least, then went on, 'and on the subject of apologies, I was out of order yesterday.'

'You certainly were,' she said crossly. 'Don't let it happen again. I know this place is like a goldfish bowl, but we're all colleagues and a bit of respect wouldn't go amiss.'

'I know. It's just...' He gave her a crooked grin that was meant to be endearing and failed. 'Well, I've always thought you were a bit special, and I was just jealous. I was rather hoping we might, ah...'

She felt her eyes widen in surprise. Mike fancied her? Good grief. She hadn't even noticed him as a man, just as an irritating and slightly incompetent colleague, and his cocky grin now was profoundly irritating. She also didn't believe a word of it. Did he really think saying that was going to get him out of trouble?

'Well, you're wasting your time because I don't mix

business with pleasure,' she told him firmly, hoping that would be enough, but she'd reckoned without the thick skin of this supremely self-confident and arrogant example of the species.

'You didn't seem to worry with Williamson yesterday,' he said with another touch of that same arrogance. It made her blood boil. Why wouldn't he just back off and drop it?

'He's a friend,' she said cuttingly. 'You're a colleague—and it's staying that way, unless you foul up so badly you lose your job. Bear it in mind.'

She turned on her heel and stalked off, walking round the corner slap into Max.

He caught her shoulders with his long, strong fingers and eased her away from him, his mouth twitching.

'Throwing yourself into my arms, precious?' he murmured, and she stepped back and laughed a little shortly.

'I've just had a run-in with Mike Taylor. He really is a pain—and he's not a good doctor.'

'I'd noticed,' Max said softly. 'What's he done now?'

So she told him, and Max frowned. 'But I wrote her up for all of that. What were the night staff doing, and what was Mike's excuse?'

'Oh, he didn't really have one, and there was an incompetent agency nurse on last night, I think, from what Damien was saying. She's been a problem before. I think he's going to report her so she's not used again. He reckons she's only doing it to gain access to drugs.'

'And we've got an incompetent SHO. Great. Want me to talk to him?'

She shook her head. 'No. I think it's OK for now. He tried to explain his behaviour yesterday, by the way—he said he fancied me himself and he was jealous! What a load of bull.'

Max chuckled. 'He's obviously made a stunning impression. I would say he's definitely in with a chance.'

'A chance of having his lights punched out. He's awful—so cocky.'

'Well, you know what they say. Pride comes before a fall—and I reckon that young man's about to topple from a great height.' He looked down at her, his eyes softening. 'So, how are you this morning?'

Annie felt the warmth of his gaze like a physical caress, and heat skittered over her skin. 'I'm fine. Alice was a bit fussy before I left, but it's the weekend now and I'm not on duty until Sunday, so I can give her my undivided attention for a day, at least.'

'How about coming out with her?' he said suddenly. 'We could do whatever she likes.'

Annie laughed, horribly tempted but quite unable to give in. 'She's only eight months old, just. She doesn't like much—food, music, cuddles—her repertoire's decidedly limited at the moment. I might take her for a walk in the park to feed the ducks. She likes to watch them.'

'That might be fun,' he said, and she had a sudden moment of panic. Max was obviously angling for an invitation to join them, and not asking him was going to sound so churlish, but she couldn't let it happen.

'Max, I think it might be better if we wait a bit,'

she said quietly. 'You know what I feel about you having too much to do with her.'

'Too much? I haven't even clapped eyes on her yet! What's the matter with her, Annie? Has she got two heads?'

Oh, lord. 'Of course not!' she said hastily. 'There's nothing the matter with her—but anyway, most of the time when I see you she's asleep.'

'Well, think about it. I promise not to bond with her or corrupt her or damage her in any way.'

His crooked smile was teasing, but she sensed it disguised his hurt, and she felt dreadful. Of course it was natural for him to want to see her, and she was probably being over-sensitive about the looks thing. Most people didn't have a clue what they looked like, and smiley, happy babies were pretty much all the same.

Weren't they?

No. Oh, heck. What a coil!

'I'll think about it,' she promised.

'Good. Got time for breakfast before we start?'

'Actually, I have,' she said a little thoughtfully. 'Although, do you really think it's a good idea? I mean, if Mike noticed we were looking rather cosy, he's probably not the only one.'

'Well, we just won't have to look too cosy, then, will we?'

Max had a steely glint in his eye and was obviously determined not to give in to Mike and his ilk. Annie gave a mental shrug. If he didn't care, why should she?

They went for breakfast.

* * *

Mrs Bradley settled down under her new drug regime, to their mutual relief, and Tim Jacobs seemed to be coping without the syringe driver, but Annie was still seething with Mike for his incompetence.

When Max was on the ward, she showed him the notes so he could see how clearly visible were the drugs he'd written up for Mrs Bradley yesterday, before he'd gone off duty.

'The man's an idiot!' Max said in disgust. 'How on earth could he not see that? It's as clear as daylight. Unless…' He peered more closely at the notes. 'These drugs that Mike's written up—I don't think that's his writing. Look, it's nothing like his signature. I wonder if the agency nurse wrote him up for the drugs, and simply got Mike to sign the form without looking at it.'

'And if so,' Annie said slowly, 'I wonder if she actually gave Mrs Bradley all she was written up for, or if she gave herself what you'd written her up for, and so couldn't let Mike see the form? She might even have had some of the pethidine Mike had signed Mrs Bradley up for.'

Max scrubbed a hand through his hair and rolled his eyes despairingly. 'It gets worse and worse. We need to speak to Damien, and then I think we probably need to involve the police. I'd better have a word with Mike first, and find out his side of the story word for word. Do you want to be there when I do that?'

Annie gave a hollow laugh. 'Do I want, or do I think I should be? Actually, I think the answer to both is "probably".'

Max called Mike into the ward office, questioned him in minute detail about exactly what had taken place during the night and then explained their concerns.

Mike, to his credit, had the grace to admit that he hadn't really studied the drug chart before signing it.

'I just accepted what she told me,' he said. 'In fact, she probably had her hand over that part of the chart, pointing to the bit where she wanted me to sign. I was tired, I was busy and I should have checked it.'

Heavens, Annie thought, humility? From Mike? Wonders will never cease.

However, his humility wasn't going to help Mrs Bradley to have had a better night, and it wasn't going to solve the problem of the agency nurse. Max called in Damien, and they checked the amount of pethidine that had been signed for in the drugs cupboard. There was less left than there should have been, and at that point they had no choice but to call in the police.

Annie phoned her mother and told her she was going to be late home. There was no way that she could leave until this had been sorted out, and the police wanted to interview her to get her version of the events.

In the end by the time she got home Alice was asleep, and Jill told her that the baby had been fussing and crying, and had taken ages to settle.

Annie crept into her daughter's darkened bedroom, and she stood at the side of her cot with tears running down her face. 'I'm sorry, baby,' she said brokenly. 'It was just one of those things. Maybe one day you'll understand and forgive me.'

The baby stirred and snuffled in her sleep, and Annie lowered the cot side, bent over and stroked a feather-light kiss over her daughter's brow. The skin felt a little hot and damp, and Annie wondered if it was a remnant from the crying or if her daughter was going down with something.

Still, she had a day off the next day, and she fully intended to spend every single moment with her daughter. She wouldn't even allow herself to think about Max, and how nice it would be to have him with them.

CHAPTER SEVEN

MAX phoned Annie at ten o'clock the following morning, and asked if she had any plans for the day.

'Yes,' she said firmly, 'I'm spending it with Alice. She wasn't well last night, and I felt really guilty when I got home so late. I've only got one day off this weekend, and it just isn't fair. She didn't ask to have a working mother.'

'I wasn't suggesting you should spend it without her,' Max said, a note of mild reproach in his voice. 'I just wondered if you fancy doing anything else—taking her somewhere, or feeding the ducks—but if she's not very well, that might not be a good idea.' He paused for a moment, then went on, 'I don't suppose you feel like having some company while you play with her?'

She did, actually. Her parents were both out for the day, and wouldn't be back until later that night, and there was nothing she wanted more than Max there to keep her company. She wanted it so much that she actually hesitated, and then she remembered her resolve.

'She's pretty grizzly,' she said, thinking as she did so that it sounded a feeble, miserable excuse. Most people with a grizzly baby would be only too happy for somebody else to come along and try and cheer it up. 'I'll probably have to walk up and down cuddling her most of the day, or trying to get her to go off to sleep, and if there's anybody else here she probably won't settle,' she continued, trying to make it plausible.

She heard Max's quiet sigh over the phone. 'OK, I understand,' he said. He sounded resigned, which was good news, actually, because Annie was rapidly reaching the point where she didn't want to argue with him any longer. The prospect of the day stretching ahead of her with no one but the fretful baby for company was depressing.

'I'm sorry,' she said with absolute sincerity. 'Maybe when she's feeling better.'

And that, of course, took away any future excuses. Never mind, because she was fast coming to the conclusion that Max was the ideal person for them both, and her good intentions seemed founded on nothing very substantial at all.

'Max, I'm sorry, I'm going to have to go because she's crying again,' Annie said regretfully.

'OK. I tell you what, ring me later if you change your mind or if she settles,' he replied. 'I should be in all day, I've got things to sort out about the house— Oh, by the way, did I tell you, my offer was accepted?'

She felt a little quiver of excitement. 'Oh, Max, that's wonderful! I'm so pleased for you.'

He gave a rueful laugh. 'I think I'm pleased for myself, but there's an awful lot of work to do and I'm feeling a bit daunted. I'm going round there again today at some point and I'm going to draw up a list of all the things that need doing and try and get them in order. By the time I've done that, I'll probably withdraw my offer!'

She could hear his smile over the phone, and it cheered her up. 'I tell you what,' she suggested, 'why don't you phone me when you get back and tell me all about it?'

'Won't I disturb the baby?'

'No, the phone is nowhere near her. It'll be fine. Max, I have to go. I'll speak to you later. Have a good day.'

She cradled the phone and ran back to Alice, scooping the miserable baby up in her arms and rocking her lovingly. 'Oh, sweetheart, what's the matter with you, darling?'

In reply, Alice scrubbed her fist against her gums and dribbled all down Annie's T-shirt.

'Oh, baby, are you teething? Grannie said you were. Come on, I'll put some gel on it for you.'

By the end of the afternoon, Annie was ready to scream. There were definite advantages to being a working mother, she'd decided. She wished Max would phone, but the instrument remained stubbornly silent.

It was probably just as well. If he phoned now and suggested he come round, she'd probably bite his hand off. But he didn't, not until seven o'clock, when Alice had finally worn herself out and fallen into a heavy sleep and Annie was slumped in a chair in her little sitting room, exhausted.

Then the phone rang, and she dragged herself out

of the chair and picked it up. 'Hello?' she said tonelessly.

'Annie?'

'Oh, hi, Max,' she said, trying to muster a little enthusiasm.

'Are you all right? You sound knackered. Have you had a really bad day?'

She rolled her eyes. 'You might say that. She's only just gone to sleep. She's been crying since I spoke to you this morning. I don't know how my mother's going to cope with her tomorrow if she's still like this.'

'Take a day off,' he suggested.

She stared at the phone in amazement. He was her boss, and he was telling her to take a day off? 'I can't, really. It's the weekend, and I'm on call, and I know it's going to be chaos. Who's going to cover it if I don't do it?'

'Me? I'm on call anyway, as back-up for you, so I might as well spend the day at work. Think about it. I've not got anything else to do, anyway, especially if you're busy.'

'Did you manage to get everything done at the house?'

He gave a choked laugh. 'Sort of. I've got a list as long as my arm—terrifying. I'm sorry it's taken me so long to come back to you, but the police wanted to speak to me again about the agency nurse. She's in deep trouble. Apparently, when they started checking back, there've been problems on several of the other wards she's worked on, and it was only when we reported things that it all began to fall into place.

Anyway, I'm finished there now, and I wondered how you were fixed. Have you eaten?'

Eaten? What was that?

'No, I haven't eaten,' she said wearily. 'I don't think I've got the strength.'

'Well, if Alice is asleep, why don't I pick up a take-away and bring it round to you, and we could share it? That way you don't have to trouble your mother to babysit, and if the baby starts to fuss you can always kick me out.'

Annie hesitated for about half a second, then succumbed. 'That would be lovely,' she said gratefully. Now she thought about it, she was absolutely starving, and the idea of having a hot tasty meal put down in front of her with absolutely no effort required on her part was wonderful.

'Any particular variety?'

'Whatever you like. I'll leave it up to you. I could eat dust at the moment.'

He chuckled. 'Don't do that. Just hang on a minute, and I'll be with you. If you leave the front door on the latch, I won't even have to ring the bell.'

'Come round the back. I've got my own door. It's in the corner, with all the pots and tubs outside. I'll leave it open.'

It took him fifteen minutes, and in that time she dived through the shower, scraped her wet hair back from her face and slapped on a little make-up—not very much, just enough to rescue her battered self-esteem.

He walked in through the door just as she put the

plates to warm in a bowl of hot water, and he had a plastic carrier bag in one hand and flowers in the other.

'Here—cheer you up a bit. You sounded really down on the phone.'

He handed her the flowers and brushed a gentle but slightly possessive kiss over her lips. It felt absolutely right. She took the flowers and buried her nose in them.

'Oh, the carnations smell gorgeous!' She went up on tiptoe and kissed his cheek. 'Thank you.'

His eyes softened. 'My pleasure,' he murmured.

She sniffed appreciatively. 'Whatever that is smells gorgeous, too.'

'Chinese. It was the first one I found, and it looked respectable.'

She looked at the name on the side of the bag and her eyebrows shot up. 'Oh, it's respectable all right. It's the best Chinese in town.' She didn't add that her family reserved them for high days and holidays. 'If I'd known you were going there, I would have laid the table and lit a candle,' she teased.

He smiled slightly. 'Sounds romantic.'

Annie felt suddenly flustered. 'I said if I'd known, but I didn't, so we'll have to eat it on our knees or it'll be cold.' She fished the plates out of the hot water, gave them a quick swipe with a tea towel, grabbed the cutlery from the drawer and headed for the sitting room with Max and his carrier bag in hot pursuit.

He put the bag down on the coffee-table, and she pulled out all the little containers, opened them and sighed. 'Bliss. Spare ribs—and lemon chicken. And Singapore noodles! Oh, I am going to be so fat.'

'I don't think so. You could do with putting on a bit of weight. You've got skinny in the past year.'

Annie rolled her eyes. 'I'm not surprised. If you'd had to run around after Alice today, you would have got skinny—and that's just one day!'

Max shook his head, and piled her plate, handing it to her with a smile. 'Here—your first course.'

She laughed. She couldn't be bothered to take offence, and anyway he was absolutely right. She fully intended to clear all the dishes before the end of the evening!

Max watched her indulgently as Annie ate her way through a vast quantity of food. He'd wondered if he was being silly and had bought far too much, but seeing the way she attacked it, he realised that she really had been hungry. He hadn't realised that she'd got her own little kitchen and sitting room at the back here, and he wondered if she did all her own cooking or if her mother helped her.

If she cooked for herself it explained a lot, because she probably didn't bother. She probably rushed in late, saw to the baby and fell onto the settee with a packet of biscuits or an apple. He resolved to bring around a take-away more often. Or, alternatively, cook for her at his house.

Now, that was a tempting thought…

Annie finally ground to a halt. Putting her plate down, she flopped back against the settee and sighed hugely.

'That was the best thing I've tasted in years,' she

said with a smile. 'I could love you for ever for the Singapore noodles.'

He gave her a curiously intent look, then his mouth quirked in a fleeting smile. 'I might just hold you to that,' he said softly, leaning over to brush her lips with his, and she felt a flood of warmth sweep through her.

It was just a figure of speech, something she would have said to anyone, but Max had turned it into something else, a declaration, and she suddenly realised that she had no urge at all to retract the innocent remark.

However, she wasn't going to follow up on it either, and she got hastily to her feet. 'Coffee?' she said brightly, and he gave her a knowing little smile.

'That would be lovely, thank you. Can I wash up while you do that?'

Annie rustled up a teasing smile. 'Goodness, house-trained as well?'

'I don't chew the furniture either,' he said, deadpan, getting to his feet and gathering together the plates and the discarded cartons.

'Amazing,' she threw over her shoulder as she walked into the kitchen. 'Whoever would have thought it? All that and beauty, too.'

As soon as the words were out of her mouth, she regretted them. Max's eyes darkened, and he followed her into the kitchen, set the plates and the bag of rubbish down, took her shoulders in his hands and turned her firmly towards him.

'I'm going to kiss you,' he said mildly. Easing her gently back up against the edge of the sink, he threaded his fingers through her hair, anchored her head with his big hands and lowered his mouth to hers.

She was helpless to resist. Well, she imagined she was. She didn't even bother to try. Instead, she just slid her arms round his waist, settled her palms against the strong column of his spine and kissed him right back.

He gave a deep groan low in his throat, and shifted closer to her, so close that nothing was left to her imagination. It was quite gratifying to know that she was driving him every bit as wild as he was driving her. The gap between them got even smaller, and their clothes were quite definitely in the way.

She was just on the point of forgetting every scrap of common sense she'd ever had when a miserable little wail cut through the haze of their passion and sobered her instantly.

'Alice,' she said unsteadily. 'Oh, damn.'

'Don't worry, you go and deal with her and I'll wash up,' he murmured. He kissed her again, just lightly on the forehead, and patted her bottom affectionately. 'Go on, scoot. I'll deal with this.'

She had no choice. Alice was wailing in earnest now, and she couldn't leave her another moment. Annie was so tired that all she wanted to do was join in, but she couldn't. Instead, she lifted the miserable baby against her shoulder and rocked her gently.

'It's all right, my darling, Mummy's here. It's all right.' She cuddled her daughter until she was calm, then put some more gel on her inflamed gum and changed her nappy. She'd hardly eaten all day, and was probably hungry, but Annie couldn't put her down again to go and get some food, and she couldn't take her into the kitchen because Max was there.

And then, just when she was utterly torn, he popped his head round the corner of the door and smiled.

'I'm going now,' he said. 'You give Alice a cuddle from me, and tell her I hope she feels better soon. And don't bother to come into work tomorrow, or I'll just send you home again.'

She stared at him over Alice's head. 'Are you sure? I'll feel so guilty...'

'Don't. Don't *ever* feel guilty for staying with your sick baby. And anyway, how guilty do you think I would feel, sitting at home with nothing to do while Alice was here crying for you and you were at work not properly paying attention and fretting yourself to death?'

She chewed her lip, instinctively rocking the still restless baby against her shoulder. 'OK, if you insist, but call me if you need me.'

'I won't—'

'Just promise, or I won't agree,' she said firmly, and he shook his head and laughed.

'OK, OK, I give in. I'll call you. Take care. Have a good day.' And with a wave of his fingers, he disappeared out of her sight.

She sighed with relief. Not only did she have the next day off with her daughter, but Max had gone before he'd seen any more than the back of Alice's head.

She went into the kitchen with Alice and made her some cereal, and while she was spooning it into her she wondered how and when she was going to tell Max about his daughter. She was stalling now, she knew that, but it was very difficult.

What was she supposed to say? 'Do you remember that time by the side of the lake? Well, guess what?'

She gave a dispirited sigh. There would be no easy way to tell him, she realised that, but she was going to have to do it, and soon, or else he was going to find out by accident and that would be a disaster.

'I wonder what he'll make of you, Tuppence?' she murmured to her baby. 'It might be nice for you to have a daddy, and I'm sure he'll be a very nice one. The thing is, how do we introduce you to him? I'm sure he'll love you to bits, but I'm not so sure how he'll feel about me. Oh, dear, Alice, what a mess.'

Annie wasn't sure if she was talking about the cereal all over her baby's face, or the coil she'd got herself into. Both, probably. Alice was at least peaceful now, so she gave her a bottle, cleaned her little teeth and popped her back into her cot before slumping onto the sofa to nurse her distended stomach and think about Max.

It was very kind of him to do the next day for her, and she was hugely grateful. It was another handful of Brownie points for him, not that he needed any more. He was already doing disgustingly well on that score.

She smiled to herself. He'd managed to earn several for his kisses, and if she closed her eyes, she could imagine herself right back in his arms…

Max turned over in bed, stared at the chirruping alarm clock in disbelief and then remembered.

He must be nuts. Oh, well, no doubt he'd get his reward in heaven. He dragged himself out of bed, sluiced rapidly in the shower and pulled on his work clothes. With any luck Suffolk would have a nice quiet day, and he'd be able to potter in his office for half of it, catching up with his admin.

Not a chance. Suffolk wasn't listening, or at least, not to him. There was a massive pile-up on the A14, and A and E were overrun. It was one of those horrendous days when they ran out of cubicles for treatment, beds were in short supply and staff even shorter.

Against his better judgement, he phoned Annie.

'How's the baby?' he asked without preamble.

'Much better. She's her usual sunny self today. I feel a real fraud.'

Max gave a hollow laugh. 'Is that right? Well, if she really is better, we could really do with your help in here. We've had a really nasty RTA and we could do with all the staff we can lay our hands on. I don't suppose there's the slightest chance your mother could help out with Alice, is there? If not, don't worry, but we are flat out. I'd be really grateful.'

She didn't even hesitate. 'Of course,' she said immediately. 'Mum was expecting to have her today anyway, so she is around. I'll just make sure. Any problems and I'll page you, but if you don't hear from me, I'll see you in about fifteen minutes.'

Max cradled the phone and heaved a quiet sigh of relief. His pager remained mercifully silent, and precisely sixteen minutes later Annie appeared at his side in A and E.

'Where do you need me?' she asked, and he shrugged.

'Everywhere. Anywhere. We've got five members

of the same family that were travelling in the people carrier, and at least three of them need fairly urgent exploratory surgery for internal injuries. The other two seen to have sustained just orthopaedic injuries, but we've got the odd fracture in our three as well, so it'll be a joint effort with the orthopods.

'And then, just to make it jolly, there are the other cars.'

Her eyes widened. 'How on earth are we going to manage? We can't possibly deal with all these people, just two of us.'

'I know that. David Armstrong and Nick Sarazin have come in, and I think I saw Owen Douglas about here earlier, but he might have gone by now. If you want to make yourself useful, you could have a look at that chap over there on the trolley. I had a quick look at him a few minutes ago, and he didn't look too bad, but just from where I'm standing he seems to have gone downhill.'

Annie walked over to the man on the trolley, shaking her head as she went. 'Heaven knows where they're all going to go,' she muttered under her breath.

'At least you know I didn't call you in under false pretences,' Max said with a grin, and she shot him a grim smile over her shoulder.

'Apparently not,' she returned.

He didn't see her again for fifteen minutes, by which time the man on the trolley had been transferred to Resus and the crash team were dealing with him.

'He needs opening up fast,' Annie told him urgently. 'I think he may have had an encapsulated bleed, and it's just reaching a critical point. If we work very fast, we might get in there and stop it before it goes. Otherwise, I don't fancy his chances. He's very shocky already.'

'Have you taken bloods for cross-matching? In fact, we'll need a whole load of tests.' He rattled off the list, but Annie was ahead of him and the tests were already under way, apparently.

'It's all done,' she assured him. 'All we need is a theatre, and somebody to open him up.'

'I think Theatre Four is free, and as for somebody to open him up, I would say you're available.'

Her jaw dropped, but then she snapped it shut and nodded. 'OK, if you really think I'm up to it.'

He gave her a reassuring wink. 'You'll be fine.'

He was in the middle of aspirating very blood-stained fluid from a middle-aged woman's abdomen to check for haemorrhaging, and when he glanced up again, Annie was gone.

He sincerely hoped that she would manage. She ought to, but without his reassuring presence she might suffer a crisis of confidence, although it would be quite unfounded. Only time would tell.

The next three hours passed in a blur. He was in Theatre Two, just opening up the last patient, when Annie appeared at his side, scrubbed and gowned and ready to assist.

He winked at her over the top of his mask. 'So how did it go?' he asked.

'OK,' she said modestly.

'That's not what I hear. I gather you were extremely cool and efficient and, according to the anaesthetist, you did a bloody good job, unquote.'

She coloured quite interestingly over the top of the mask, but her eyes were laughing. 'Is it insubordinate to call you a rat, sir?' she said very quietly, for his ears only, but Moira's eyes widened involuntarily.

He suppressed a grin.

'Credit where it's due, Dr Shaw,' he said mildly. 'Now, are you going to stand there bragging all day, or are you going to help me? Because if you are, you might hold that retractor for me in a rather better position.'

It was more than five hours from Max's phone call before she got home again, and to her enormous relief Alice was fed and bathed and gurgling happily on her grandfather's knee.

'Hello, darling,' he said, shooting her a keen look. 'How was it? You look tired.'

'I am tired. I'm very tired, but it went really well, and we didn't lose anybody.'

Her father nodded approvingly. 'Good, good. That's always gratifying, although you have to remember you're only human and anyway it may not be your fault if they die. Sometimes they have to take responsibility for that themselves.'

She sat down on the settee beside him and kissed Alice. 'So how's my baby?' she asked, and was rewarded with a juicy raspberry.

She laughed and wiped the fine spray of spit off her face. 'That good, eh?' She reached out her arms and Alice squirmed into them, hanging onto her hair to steady herself as she stood up and bounced up and down on Annie's lap.

Alice laughed, and for an instant she was so like Max that Annie's smile faltered. Soon, she promised herself.

Very soon.

She scooped the baby up and got to her feet, bending over to kiss her father goodnight. 'Time for bed, young lady,' she said firmly, and carried Alice through to their little flat.

She went down with scarcely a protest, and within five minutes she was sound asleep.

Annie made herself a cup of tea and curled up in front of the television with a packet of biscuits and the Sunday paper. She had hardly scanned the headlines before the phone rang beside her, and it was Max.

'How are things?' he asked.

'Fine,' she assured him. 'I'm tired, but, then, I expect you are, too. It was pretty chaotic in there today, wasn't it?'

His chuckle was wry. 'You might say that,' he said dryly, and then his voice softened. 'I don't suppose you've got the energy for a little stroll around the block, have you? My body feels full of kinks and knots, and a bit of mindless repetitive action is just what it needs before I go to sleep.'

'All mine needs is a stiff whisky,' she said with a chuckle. 'But I expect I can manage. Shall I meet you out the front in a minute?'

'I'll be straight round.'

She pulled on a thin jumper, because although the August days were warm, it was beginning to chill off at night. Then she stuck her head round her parents' sitting-room door and asked them to keep an ear out for Alice.

'I won't be more than a few minutes,' she promised, but judging by the look her parents exchanged, they wouldn't have cared if she'd been out all night, so long as it was with Max!

CHAPTER EIGHT

THE hospital was absolutely heaving after the hectic events of the previous day. Their patients seemed to be spread around the hospital, with surgical beds tucked into medical wards, geriatric wards and anywhere else a slot could be found.

People were wandering around muttering about bed blocking under their breath, but for Annie all it meant was that she had to run from one end of the hospital to the other to check on them all. Mike, who had been away for the weekend, was closeted for most of the morning with the police, and so most of the responsibility for the patients fell to Annie.

Max was in Theatre, working his way steadily through the elective list, and Annie was just hoping that there would be somewhere for them to go when they came back down from Recovery. They were all allocated beds, but if another emergency arose they would be extremely pushed for space.

Max came down halfway through his list, while they were scrubbing out Theatre, and found Annie propped up in the kitchen, gulping down a mug of coffee.

He gave her a crooked grin, checked over his shoulder that no one was looking, and dropped a quick kiss on her lips. 'Any chance of a sip of that?'

She handed him the mug with a smile. 'How's it going?' she asked.

'Oh, you know, some of it's taken longer, some of it's been quicker. I had a tricky bowel resection—I could have done with your help. How's Alice?'

Annie's smile widened. 'She has a new tooth!' she said proudly.

'Well, thank goodness for that. Now you might be able to get some sleep.'

'And come to work when I'm supposed to. Thank you very much for doing yesterday for me.'

Max shrugged. 'In the end, of course, it didn't make a great deal of difference, because I would have been here anyway. How's the bed situation?' he added, and Annie rolled her eyes.

'Dire,' she told him bluntly. 'We've got one in Geriatrics, two on a medical ward, and even one in the side room of a children's ward. I tell you what, I won't be needing any exercise today.'

Max chuckled. 'It's good for you. It'll get you in training.'

'In training for what?' she asked indignantly. 'I don't need to be in training for anything!'

Max's eyes twinkled, and with a muffled chuckle, she punched his arm lightly.

'In your dreams,' she said, and he gave a wry laugh.

'Oh, absolutely—every single night.'

She felt her skin warm at the heat in his eyes, and looked away quickly before her own eyes gave her away.

She was too late, however, because Max groaned softly under his breath and said, 'Don't look at me like that, or I'll have to put a white coat on over my scrubs to cover up the evidence.'

'Nothing to do with me,' she said primly, and headed for the door. 'You'd better stay in here and count sheep or something until you settle down!'

His smothered laugh followed her out of the room, and with a smile on her face she headed back towards the geriatric ward to review the pain relief for their patient there. She was about halfway when her bleeper squawked, and she groaned to herself. If she had to go all the way back to the surgical ward, she'd scream!

She went to the nearest phone and called the switchboard, and they put her through to Max.

'You are a sexy little witch,' he said with a thread of laughter in his voice.

Annie hid her smile. 'I don't know what you're talking about.'

'Is that right? So why are you smiling? I can hear it in your voice. I think you need punishing for being so unkind to me. You can come round to mine tonight for dinner. I'll cook for you, and if you're very lucky it'll be edible.'

She felt her heart thump at the thought of being alone with him, and remembered she hadn't yet been to the clinic. 'I'll have to check with Mum,' she said. 'I'll let you know.'

'You do that. Where are you?'

'On my way to Geriatrics to see our patient. He's apparently in a lot of pain.'

'Call me if you need me,' he said, and hung up. She carried on up the endless miles of corridor, and all she could think of on the way was spending the evening with Max.

Max took a stroll outside at lunchtime to get the kinks out of his neck and back from hours of operating, and his feet took him past an entrance.

SEXUAL HEALTH AND FAMILY PLANNING CLINIC, it announced cheerfully, and he remembered he still hadn't acquired the wherewithal to organise any precautions. He hesitated by the door for a moment, and then to his surprise Annie came out, stopped dead at the sight of him and blushed scarlet.

'Hi,' he said gently, searching her suddenly evasive eyes.

'What are you doing here?' she asked a little frantically.

'The same as you, maybe,' he replied, a slow smile touching his mouth. 'Just to be on the safe side.'

She seemed to relax, then she gave a soft huff of laughter. 'Of all the people to run into…'

'I take it your visit was for my benefit and no one else's?' he asked, suddenly wondering if he was jumping the gun and assuming too much.

'Of course! What do you think I am?'

'Wonderful. Beautiful. Intelligent. Well organised, sexy, the star feature in every one of my dreams for the last year and a bit—'

'You're silly,' she muttered, her colour rising again.

'No. Only about you.'

Annie met his eyes, and her own softened and mellowed. He groaned again and rammed his hands into the pockets of his white coat, using it as a shield. He was going to have to do something about this adolescent reaction he had to her every time he saw her!

'Did you ring your mother?' he asked, and she nodded.

'Yes, she's fine with it. What time would you like me?'

Max's mouth opened, and he just stopped himself from saying, Now!

'Seven?' he suggested. 'Seven-thirty? Whatever.'

'Sounds good. Are you on your way to your clinic?'

He nodded. 'Yes. You're there as well, aren't you? Have the police finished with Mike Taylor, or is he still out of action? If so, I might have to do without you for the clinic.'

'He's back,' she told him. 'So you get the pleasure of my company.'

'Wonderful. We should be able to get through them at a sensible speed, then. Have you had lunch?'

She nodded. 'Well, a bit of birthday cake on the children's ward. It'll do me. I'm going to go and bed-shuffle. Can Tim Jacobs go home? He's looking fine now.'

'If he's careful. I'd like to see him in a week.'

'OK. I'll go and discharge him and free up his bed, and then I'll see you in the clinic.'

'OK.'

She smiled at him with that wonderful too-wide mouth, and he felt desire hit him again in his midsection. He was going to have a hell of a job keeping his hands off her tonight!

Annie walked back to the ward, all too conscious of the little foil packets in her pocket next to the first three months' supply of the Pill. She could start taking it today, and would need additional protective cover for the next seven days, so she'd been told.

If necessary.

Her heart thumped against her ribs, and she swallowed hard, her mouth suddenly dry with anticipation.

Would it be necessary tonight? Max was certainly turning up the heat, and her ability to resist him was so slight as to be not worth mentioning. The chances seemed quite high.

And knowing this, she had to get through the afternoon clinic with him!

Max laid the table in the dining-room, overlooking the back garden, and as it was a lovely evening he thought they could open the French windows while they ate. He hadn't opened them yet, though, because he didn't want the neighbourhood cats marauding about all over the table.

As he left the room, he gave it one last critical glance. The glasses were polished, the silverware was gleaming, and the roses were ones he'd pinched from the front garden of what would be his new house. They were beautiful, a dark, rich red, and the scent was phenomenal. He'd put candles on the table, but he wouldn't light them until Annie had arrived.

The dining-room would do, but he was less certain about the meal. He'd kept it deliberately simple, with salmon steaks marinated in lime and coriander, minted new potatoes and a selection of baby vegetables—sweetcorn, asparagus tips and mange-tout.

He hadn't been able to get Hollandaise sauce at the deli, so he'd bought a lime and sliced it to squeeze over the salmon. Pudding was a bought chocolate gateau, with lashings of cream, and he'd piled fresh raspberries on top to liven it up a bit.

If she was still hungry—and knowing Annie, he wouldn't be surprised—then he had some lovely farmhouse Cheddar and a bit of Brie so ripe it was threatening to run away.

And, of course, wine. He'd remembered that she only liked white, and he'd chosen a delightfully fruity muscat which was chilling in the fridge.

All he had to do now was not burn the salmon, not boil the potatoes to mush and not ruin the baby vegetables by cooking them to death.

Three more things to add to his long list of nots.

He was not to push her too hard, he was not to assume that just because he'd caught her coming out of the clinic she was necessarily in a hurry to sleep with him tonight, he was not to talk her into doing anything she didn't feel ready to do, he was not to kiss her senseless the moment she walked through the door, he was not to act like a sex-crazed teenager and embarrass either of them.

The list was endless, and seemed to revolve entirely around his hyperactive libido. Not that it was necessarily that hyperactive. It had been fifteen months now since he'd met Annie, and there had been no one since—she'd been too hard an act to follow. It was probably no wonder that he was feeling a little hyperactive.

He glanced at his watch. Ten to seven. He just had time for a quick shower before she arrived.

Running upstairs he yanked off his clothes and showered rapidly. He was just pulling on his trousers and tucking in his shirt when the doorbell rang, and he ran downstairs to let her in, his feet still bare, half his buttons not yet done up, and her eyes widened with surprise.

'Sorry, am I too early?' she said, her eyes scanning him with what looked suspiciously like hunger.

'Absolutely not,' he said. Drawing her inside, he pulled her into his arms and kissed her. She tasted of toothpaste, and her hair smelt of that lovely shampoo she'd always used, and for a minute he totally forgot himself.

Then he remembered his list of nos, and lifted his head. 'I wasn't going to do that,' he confessed, 'but you just look so gorgeous.'

Annie laughed softly. 'You're such a liar. Some people will go to any lengths to get a kiss.'

'It's not a lie,' he said. 'You do look gorgeous tonight. You always look gorgeous.'

'I don't in the morning.'

'I wouldn't know, I've never been there to see you, but I have my doubts. Remind me to check it out one day soon.'

Her eyes flared, and he could see an aching need in their vulnerable and revealing depths. It was like looking in a mirror.

He looked away. 'Come on through to the kitchen, I'll get you a drink while I cook the supper,' he said.

She sniffed, and tilted her head at him. 'Have you started it yet?'

'No. It's all quick stuff—well, except for the new potatoes. They take a few minutes longer than the rest.'

'Is the menu a secret?' she asked, and he chuckled.

'No, not at all, although that's a good idea. Then if I wreck it, I can pretend we were always having tinned tuna with oven chips, can't I?'

She laughed. 'So, not that, then, unless it's a disaster.'

'No, but it is fish. Salmon.'

'Oh, lovely,' she said spontaneously. 'I adore salmon.'

'I know. I remember. You had it at the hotel, the night before—well, the night before.'

Hell. He hadn't meant to bring it up again, because every time he thought about it, the more difficult it grew to forget and put it in the past. And now she was looking at him with wide haunted eyes and her lips slightly parted, and a deep, slow ache started to build inside him.

He cleared his throat and looked away. 'Anyway, it's salmon, and new potatoes and baby veg—if I don't trash it.'

'You won't,' she said confidently. 'I promise not to distract you.'

He gave a rude snort of laughter. She always distracted him. Just having her there on the bar stool watching was such a distraction he was likely to burn the house down, never mind overcook the salmon!

*   *   *

The food was wonderful. Max had cooked it beautifully, and all she'd had to do was sit quietly and watch him, which had been absolutely no hardship at all.

They ate in the dining-room, with the French doors open into the pretty little garden, and there were roses on the table which he confessed were from his new house, and the glasses and tableware were gleaming in the candlelight.

He'd gone to a great deal of trouble to set the scene, she thought. If only he'd realised how unnecessary it all was, because she'd made up her mind on the way over here that it was time to move things on in their relationship, so all the window-dressing and scene-setting were a little superfluous.

Unless—no. It was far too soon, just wishful thinking. He was just pampering her, she thought with a twinge of disappointment.

Still, it was nice to feel pampered, she told herself, and she settled back and enjoyed it.

The wine was mellow and fruity, just the sort of thing she liked, and, of course, he knew that, just as he'd known she liked salmon. It was another thoughtful little touch, and she probably had rather more than was sensible if she wanted to keep her head.

Annie visualised the little shelf of things she'd put on one side carefully to show him—Alice's baby photos from the time of her birth, a video, her first tiny little all-in-one suit that had drowned her—all the things she wished he'd been there to see and that he'd missed. She was going to tell him tonight, after dinner, and take him home to show him.

She'd even changed the sheets—just in case.

And then he offered her a glass of dessert wine with the wickedly sticky chocolate gateau and raspberries, and she made herself sip it carefully. She wanted to keep a clear head, because she knew if she told him about Alice that tonight was going to be hugely significant—possibly the most important night of her life.

'Any more?' he asked, waving the knife at the gateau, but she shook her head.

'No, thank you, Max, that was lovely. Have it for breakfast.'

He gave an abrupt little laugh and got to his feet. 'Um, I've put the coffee on. Why don't you go into the sitting room? We'll leave this lot, I'll deal with it tomorrow.'

He shut the French doors, grabbed the half-eaten gateau and the jug of cream and disappeared, leaving her staring after him in confusion. Was she just imagining it, or had he seemed tense and a little…nervous?

Max, nervous? Whatever for?

Unless…

She shrugged and went obediently into the sitting room with the remains of her dessert wine. Soft music was playing, and there were more roses on the coffee-table, next to a box of mint crisps.

She loved mint crisps. She picked one up and settled herself into the corner of the sofa, her feet curled under her bottom, and nibbled the chocolate and sipped the wine while she waited for him.

He wasn't long. He came in, set the tray down on the coffee-table and poured the coffee, then sat down at the other end of the sofa. He seemed a long way away, so she unravelled her legs and turned sideways, tucking her toes under his thigh.

His hand came down instantly and curled over her feet, his thumb grazing the bare skin in a soothing, rhythmic gesture she wasn't sure he was even aware of. He seemed distracted, and she prodded him with her toes.

'Smile,' she commanded. 'That was a lovely meal, you can relax now. I have to say I didn't realise you were such a good cook or I wouldn't have settled for beans on toast last time.'

He smiled, a crooked little quirk of his mouth, then his face sobered and his eyes locked with hers.

'You seem a long way away,' he murmured, and she smiled.

'I was just thinking that,' she admitted, and wriggled closer, close enough that he could wrap his arm round her shoulders and tuck her up against his side.

'That's better,' he said, and she could feel the tension in him. His body was all but humming with it, and she found she was picking it up.

She tilted her head slightly to one side and looked up at him, trying to read his expression. 'Max, what's wrong?' she asked softly.

He looked down into her eyes. 'Nothing's wrong,' he said, but his voice seemed taut somehow. He hesitated, then added, 'I've got a feeling I'm about to make a complete fool of myself, that's all.'

He eased his arm away, stood up and plucked one of the roses from the vase, wiped the wet stem and turned towards her. She thought he was going to give it to her, but instead he went down on one knee and held it out to her, his eyes locked with hers, and her heart thumped and skittered against her ribs. Oh, Max…

'I love you, Annie,' he said, his voice shaking slightly. 'I know you've had a hell of a year, and I know I haven't helped, and I know it's too soon, but I do love you. I've loved you since I first saw you in the doorway at the hotel. I don't know what it was, I just connected with you, and nothing's been the same for me since.'

He hesitated, but when she opened her mouth to speak he shook his head and put a finger over her lips. 'No. Let me finish. I've got this far.'

He swallowed and looked away, then looked back, and his eyes were blazing with need and longing and something she'd never seen before.

Love, she realised dimly. Real love, the sort of love that nothing can destroy.

'Marry me, Annie,' he said, his voice crackling with emotion. 'Please? Come and live with me in my new house and help me prune the roses and mend the swing for Alice, and then maybe one day there'll be another Alice—'

He broke off, and Annie slowly and carefully took the rose from his trembling hands. 'I'd love to marry you,' she said, her heart overflowing, 'but before I say yes, there are things you must know. Things I haven't told you. One thing, anyway.'

'Just tell me this first,' he said urgently. 'Do you love me?'

She felt the smile split her face in two. 'Oh, yes.

Oh, yes, Max, I love you. I couldn't have got through the last year without you there in my heart.'

'Oh, Annie…'

He gathered her into his arms. 'That's all I need to know,' he said, and his mouth found hers in a searing kiss that left her breathless. When he finally came up for air, his eyes were blazing with desire, and heat rocketed through her.

'Max?' she whispered, and with a ragged groan he kissed her again. Without lifting his mouth from hers, he scooped her up in his arms and carried her up the stairs to his bedroom.

'I wasn't going to do this,' he muttered, and lowered her to her feet, sliding her down his front so she could feel every intimate inch of him. His lips found hers again, his hands tunnelling through her hair and anchoring her head while his tongue plundered the depths of her mouth.

'Annie,' he groaned unsteadily, and then he was stepping back a fraction, looking at her with eyes of fire.

'You are so beautiful,' he said.

She laughed uneasily. 'No, I'm not. I've got mud-coloured eyes and my mouth's too big—'

'So is Julia Roberts's, and you show me a man who doesn't think it's the sexiest thing he's ever seen—and your eyes aren't mud-coloured, they're a wonderful green.'

'You're besotted.' She laughed, still shy, and he shook his head slowly.

'No. Just in love. Undress for me,' he ordered softly. With her heart pounding, she pulled her top over her head, slid down her silk trousers so that they puddled at her feet and stepped out of them.

'Your turn,' she said, and he undid his shirt buttons slowly, one at a time, making her wait while all the time his eyes burned into her and set her on fire.

Finally his shirt hit the floor, and he unbuckled his belt, slipped the catch on his trousers and slid the zip down with irritating slowness.

His trousers fell to his ankles and he kicked them aside, then hooked off his briefs and straightened up.

Her breath caught and she swallowed hard and closed her eyes. She'd never seen him naked, and she felt suddenly unsure. He seemed so big and male and—well, beautiful, really, lean and honed and perfect. She wondered what he'd say when she took her bra off and her breasts slid towards her ankles. She couldn't compete with that sort of perfection.

'Annie?'

She opened her eyes, and he was standing right in front of her, just inches away.

'Darling, what's wrong?'

Inexplicably her eyes filled with tears. 'I've had a baby. I don't look like I used to.'

'You look fine to me.'

'You can't see me yet. I breast-fed her till last month. I sag.'

He laughed softly and grazed her cheek with his knuckles. 'You're lovely. You aren't meant to look like a pert teenager, you're a mother. If you weren't a mother now, you would be soon, so if I can't handle it perhaps we need to know.'

He was smiling gently at her, teasing her, and with

a resigned sigh she unfastened the catch on her bra and pulled it off. His hands were there ready to catch her breasts as they spilled free, and with infinite tenderness he bent his head and brushed a kiss over her lips, then over the pale swell of each breast in turn.

Then he lifted his head and stared deep into her eyes. 'I want you, Annie,' he said gruffly. 'I don't think I can wait any more. I've waited so long.'

She went into his arms with a little cry of need, and he lifted her and put her down gently in the centre of the bed, kneeling beside her. He looked down at her, his eyes darkening, and with gentle hands he stripped away the little lacy knickers she'd worn specially, just in case, then bent his head and brushed a kiss over the damp curls.

She felt the warm sigh of his breath and a little cry broke free in her throat.

'Max, please, hold me,' she pleaded, and then he was beside her, his arms wrapped around her, cradling her against his chest.

'I need you, Annie. I can't wait,' he said, and then swore softly. 'Hang on. Don't go anywhere.'

He rolled over, opened the drawer of the bedside cabinet and she heard something tear. Seconds later he was back, his hand sliding down and finding her aching centre with devastating accuracy.

She bucked under his hand, crying out, and with a savage groan he moved over her and entered her in one smooth, slow thrust that sent her over the brink.

'Yes!' he whispered harshly, and then he was there with her, riding the crest of the wave until they came gently back to earth.

Her heart was pounding, her body was trembling from end to end and she just wanted to weep with happiness.

Max raised himself up on his elbows and stared down at her, his face stunned. 'Dear God,' he whispered reverently. 'I'd forgotten just how incredible it was with you. Oh, Annie, I love you.'

His shoulders heaved, and he gathered her fiercely into his arms and crushed her against his chest. 'I love you so much,' he said raggedly. 'I thought I'd lost you for ever. I thought I'd be alone for the rest of my life, and now I've got you and Alice.'

He broke off, his arms convulsing around her, and Annie pressed her lips against his tear-drenched cheek and hugged him back. 'I know just how you feel. I could never even think about anyone but you. I thought it was going to be just me and the baby, and I needed you so much—'

Her voice faltered and she buried her face in the hollow of his shoulder and clung to him until the tears stopped falling.

Then he lifted his head and looked down into her eyes, and kissed her with devastating tenderness. 'Are you all right now?' he asked gently, and she nodded.

'You?'

Max's grin was crooked. 'Oh, I think I'll manage.' His grin faded and he kissed her again. 'I'm sorry, I'm not used to letting my emotions out like that, but they just wouldn't stay put.'

'They shouldn't,' she assured him. 'Not with me. You're allowed to let go when you're with me. I'd feel cheated if you didn't.'

He laughed. 'I don't think you need feel cheated,' he said wryly. 'I don't seem to have a choice but to let go.' He rolled away from her and sat up, his legs over the edge of the bed. 'I'm going to get the coffee and the chocolates. Why don't you climb into the bed and make yourself comfortable?'

He appeared a few minutes later, clad in a ratty old towelling dressing-gown, the tray balanced on one hand. He set it down on the bedside table, shucked off the dressing-gown and got in beside her, then turned to her with a smile.

'Right. Here's your coffee, here are the chocolates, and now you can tell me what you were trying to say downstairs before I talked you into bed.'

Her heart thumped against her ribs, and she took the coffee and stared down into it. It was cool now, the cream congealing on the top, but she had a sip anyway, just to give her a few seconds to find the right words.

Finally she gave up, put the coffee down and turned to face him.

'It's about Alice,' she said bluntly. 'She's your daughter.'

CHAPTER NINE

MAX was stunned. Whatever he'd expected, it hadn't been this. He searched Annie's face, wondering if he'd misunderstood, but there was nothing there to indicate that he had.

'Mine?' he said numbly. 'Alice is *mine*?'

'Yes. She looks just like you.'

'But—she's eight months old. She can't be mine. Eight and nine is seventeen months, not fifteen. We met fifteen months ago. She can't be mine,' he repeated.

'She was premature. They thought she was small for dates, because of all the trauma with Peter and everything, but when she was born she was definitely prem, about thirty-three weeks gestation, so I knew straight away she couldn't have been his, because we hadn't—'

She broke off, shrugging helplessly, and he felt something inside him ease a little. Thank God for small mercies, he thought bitterly. He'd had a hard time dealing with the fact that she'd been pregnant with Peter's child when he'd made love to her, and now he discovered she couldn't have been.

In a curiously painful way, that was comforting.

She went on in an odd, flat little voice, 'He hadn't felt really well for some time, and the holiday was supposed to help him get better and maybe liven up our flagging marriage. He just thought he was exhausted but, of course, he wasn't. So, anyway, I knew she couldn't be his, and as soon as she opened her eyes I knew for sure.'

'Why didn't you tell me?'

'Why?' she asked, sounding puzzled. 'I didn't know till she was born that she was yours and, anyway, I thought you were married.'

'You still should have contacted me,' he insisted.

Annie shook her head. 'How could I? Your relationship with Fiona seemed strained enough, and I didn't know your surname, far less your address. How was I supposed to contact you?'

'Via the hotel? They had my address.'

'And say what? Oh, hello, hope your marriage is going well, and by the way, we've had a baby? Don't be silly! And anyway, we'd agreed that that was the end of it, just that one day. I couldn't contact you without breaking our agreement, and for some stupid reason that seemed important to me.'

Max looked away, swallowing hard. She had a point, of course, but then now, for the last week…

'Why didn't you tell me when you saw me again?' he asked, but she looked away, suddenly evasive, and he saw red.

'You weren't going to, were you?' he said slowly, his temper rising with his voice. 'You weren't going to tell me at all. My God, all that rubbish about her not getting attached to me—it was all just so much hogwash! You just didn't want me to see her in case I realised she was mine!'

He threw off the quilt and shot out of bed, snagging

his dressing-gown off the floor and shoving his arms ruthlessly into it. He belted it tightly and rammed his hands into his pockets, then stood at the window staring out over the darkened garden and struggling with his temper.

'Max, please, don't be like this,' she pleaded, but he was deaf to the appeal in her voice. It was drowned out by the sound of the cogs grinding round in his head, and then suddenly everything fell into place.

'If I hadn't asked you to marry me,' he said slowly, 'you wouldn't have told me, would you? You would have kept it from me, and you've got no right to do that. She's my child, Annie. I had a right to know about her, and you were going to keep it from me.'

'No! I was going to tell you tonight. I've got all the stuff ready.'

'Stuff?' He turned round, glaring at her as she sat huddled on the bed, her eyes huge in her pale face. 'What stuff?'

'Photos, her first sleep-suit—all sorts of things. I was going to ask you to come back with me, but then we ended up here. Max, please, don't be angry. I had to be sure—'

'Sure?' he said, totally confused now. 'Sure of what?'

'Of you. Sure that you would be good to her, that you really wanted me for myself and not just for her, sure that you weren't just a promiscuous philanderer and didn't care about anything but yourself.'

Promiscuous philanderer? It was so far off the mark it was almost funny, but he wasn't laughing.

'That, coming from you, just takes the biscuit,' he muttered.

'Excuse me?'

'You heard,' he snapped. 'For God's sake, you were married.'

'And you were engaged! Don't try landing me with that one, we were both in the same position as far as commitment is concerned. We were both equally at fault.'

He scrubbed a hand through his hair and sighed harshly. 'Whatever, that doesn't alter the present. Now I have a daughter that I've only ever caught a glimpse of once, and I reckon there's a good chance I would never have known about her at all, because you had to put me through some sort of stupid *test*?'

Annie slumped against the headboard, her arms wrapped tightly round her waist, and shook her head in denial. 'Try and see it from my point of view, Max. I didn't know you—not really. Not enough. I had to be sure. She's so precious, I couldn't take risks with her—surely you understand that? You would have done the same if she'd been yours.'

'She *is* mine!' he growled, and the last vestige of his control snapped.

'Oh, get out!' he said, ramming his hands through his hair in frustration. 'Just get dressed and get out. I don't want you here—not now, maybe not ever. I don't know. I need to think. Just, please, go.'

He turned away, hardening himself to the sound of Annie's muffled crying as she dressed hastily. He heard something rip, and a little sob, and then she was going, her bare feet running down the stairs. Moments later the front door banged shut behind her, and he felt the tension drain from his shoulders.

Max slumped against the window-frame, staring sightlessly down into the garden. He could see the path in the light spilling from the kitchen window, but then it went hazy and started to swim, and he blinked angrily and slammed his hand against the wall, just catching the edge of the window-frame with his knuckle.

Pain shot through it, but he ignored it and headed for the stairs, taking the untouched coffee-tray with him. There was a foil wrapper on the floor near the door from the condom he'd used, and he kicked it viciously across the room before going down.

Pity he hadn't thought about that before, he thought disgustedly. It could have saved them both a great deal of grief, and then he wouldn't have had this to deal with.

He slammed the tray down in the kitchen and yelped. His hand was agony. He looked at it, and gingerly prodded it. There was nothing much to feel, but when he got hold of the end of his ring finger and wiggled it, he felt bones grate sickeningly.

He sat down abruptly on the bar stool and nursed it against his chest. Damn. He'd broken it. He'd broken a bone in his hand, and his right hand at that, so he wouldn't be able to operate for days, maybe weeks.

Steve Kelly was already busy enough, without taking on his work, and he couldn't trust Mike Taylor to sew on a button, which meant Annie, and because she hadn't sat any of her surgical exams yet he would have to oversee all her work.

Which would mean being with her every time they had to operate, training her, watching her every move, smelling her perfume, wanting her despite his better judgement, having his heart flayed raw because he was such a fool.

She could have just told him about the baby, but she'd obviously been hanging on for the big prize, marriage to a consultant. She'd done it once, why not do it again?

His logic was confused, he knew, but it was too close to home for him to analyse it, and anyway, it was all too familiar. Another Fiona, he thought bitterly, and tears of anger and hurt and disappointment stung his eyes.

Well, not now, he vowed to himself. He wouldn't marry her now if she were the last woman in the world!

And he would fight her for his daughter...

He'd got a spiral fracture of the fourth metacarpal. It was spectacularly pretty on X-ray, and Matt Jordan was suitably jovial about it.

'That's a classic boxer's injury,' he said with a grin. 'What were you doing, punching someone's lights out?'

'You don't want to know,' Max growled. 'How the hell am I going to operate?'

'You aren't,' he was told bluntly. 'Not for a week or two, at least. I'll need to put a nerve block in your hand to reduce it, then strap it up. Maybe a cast, maybe a splint—depends how sensible you are with it and how stable it is.'

'Can't you just pull it?'

Matt's eyebrows shot up. 'Just like that, without an anaesthetic? I can. I'd rather not. You'll probably yell the place down.'

'Oh, for God's sake, man, it's not a Colles' fracture, it's only a damn finger. Just do it,' Max said heavily. 'Just pull the damn thing straight and let's get on with it. I don't want any anaesthetic and I don't want a load of fuss. I have to go to work.'

Matt shrugged. 'OK, if you insist. Just don't say I didn't warn you.'

He got hold of the end of Max's finger, counted down from three and then gave it a sharp tug and twist. Fire shot up Max's arm, and he grunted with pain and clamped his teeth together hard.

Matt ran his finger down the back of Max's hand and nodded. 'Very good. You didn't scream. Right, don't move it, let's have another picture.'

Thankfully it was in place, because for all his silence Max didn't think he could really face having it pulled again. Matt strapped it to a splint, garter-strapped the finger to the adjacent one and sent him on his way with painkillers and strict instructions, most of which he fully intended to ignore.

He went up to the ward and, as luck would have it, the first person he ran into was Annie, looking chalk white and blotchy with red-rimmed eyes.

Guilt stabbed at him, but he dismissed it. She was the one who should be feeling guilty.

Then she caught sight of the strapping on his hand, and her eyes widened. 'Max? What have you done?' she whispered.

'I broke a bone.'

'What? How? Why?'

'Why? I hit something with it,' he said bluntly, and she closed her eyes and gave a ragged little sigh.

'Oh,' she said weakly. 'I thought—for a moment—I'm sorry. After Peter…'

Of course, fractures were particularly significant for her. Still, that wasn't his problem. 'Bad luck,' he said a little harshly. 'You don't get rid of me that easily. I hit it good and hard.'

'Good,' she said, with a rallying of her old spirit. 'I hope it hurt like hell.'

'It did, actually.'

'Excellent. Excuse me, I have work to do.'

Max put his arm up to block her way. 'Not before we've spoken.'

'I have nothing to say to you,' she said coldly. 'Anything I might have said—'

'I am your boss,' he said, pulling rank in a way that made him extremely uncomfortable but just then seemed the only way to deal with the situation. 'I want to talk to you about work. We need to make arrangements to cover my theatre time until this heals. That means you, I'm afraid. I can't operate, but I can supervise, and you can learn.'

As the ramifications of that sank in, Annie paled and closed her eyes. 'Fine. Just tell me when and where.'

'I will—and the rest of the time, I suggest you make yourself scarce. And I want to see Alice. I'll come round tonight at seven.'

'She goes to bed at seven.'

'So I'll come at six.'

'She has supper then, and her bath.'

'So I'll feed her and bath her. She might as well get used to me. And don't bother to be there. I'll deal with your mother.'

She snorted. 'You'd be safer dealing with me. Maternal instinct is a dangerous thing—and anyway, there's no way you're touching my daughter without me being there. Now, if you'll excuse me, I have work to do.'

Annie turned on her heel and walked away, her heart breaking. She'd cried all night, sobbing into her pillow so she didn't disturb Alice, and then over breakfast she'd managed to convince herself that Max just needed time for the news to sink in and he'd be fine. By the time he got to work the storm would have blown itself out and he'd be calm again and willing to talk to her.

Or not, she thought bitterly. Oh, Max, why? You stubborn idiot. Why can't you see it?

She turned the corner and went straight into David Armstrong's chest.

'Oops—Annie?' He held her at arm's length, peered at her tear-stained face and tutted gently. 'What is it?'

'Max,' she said unsteadily, and then she was cradled against David's big, solid chest and he was comforting her like a child.

'Come on, let's get out of the corridor,' he said, and led her into the day room, empty at that time of day. 'Now, tell Uncle David all about it.'

'Oh, hell, I can't. It's too complicated.'

'Work or personal?'

'Personal.'

'You knew each other before, didn't you?' he said softly.

Annie nodded. 'Yes. We met last year. We didn't really get to know each other, but...we were getting on so well, but now...' She sighed. 'It's just a stupid misunderstanding, but I just can't get through to him, and he's so angry with me.'

'Been there, done that,' he murmured. 'Julia and I did exactly the same thing last Christmas, then something happened that forced us to work together, and we realised just how much we meant to each other.' He hesitated for a moment, then said, 'Do you want me to talk to him?'

'No! He won't listen to you, and I don't want to air our laundry in public, if you don't mind. Oh, that's sounds awful,' she said tearfully, 'and it's not that I'm not grateful, but it's just so personal, we have to sort it out ourselves.'

'OK.' He squeezed her shoulders. 'Will you be all right now? I have to go and see my patients before I start my list, and I'm on the drag as it is. Julia was feeling a bit rough this morning and I didn't like to leave her until I was sure she was all right. The baby's due in a few weeks and she's finding it all a bit much.'

'I'll be fine. I hope she's OK. Thanks, David.'

'My pleasure. You take care—and if there's anything I can do, just holler.'

'I will. Thanks.'

She smiled, probably a pretty weak effort but it was the best she could do. After he'd gone out, she sluiced her face at the basin in the corner and blotted it dry, casting a despairing glance at the mirror in passing.

She looked awful—hideously unprofessional, apart from any other consideration—but it would take more than make-up to cover the ravages of the night.

Especially if she kept on topping up the effect throughout the day, as she seemed to be doing.

Oh, damn.

She straightened her shoulders and dragged in a huge breath. She could do it. She'd be fine. She'd get through the day—somehow.

Her bleeper called her, and she was summoned to the geriatric ward where their patient from Sunday was going downhill. He'd been the one she'd operated on alone, the one with the encapsulated bleed that had finally started to leak just before she'd opened him up, and she'd thought she'd done everything necessary.

Now it looked as if he needed to go back to Theatre urgently, and she didn't know what to do about it. Steve Kelly was on a day off, Mike Taylor was totally inexperienced and that left her and Max.

Oh, great.

She examined the patient's abdomen, checked his charts again, felt his pulse, thin and rapid and definitely not right, and gave him a reassuring smile.

'Well, Mr Andrews, I'm afraid you're going to have to go to Theatre again. You seem to have another problem that's developed, so I'll get you prepped and up there as soon as possible. Do you feel up to signing the consent form for me?'

He nodded weakly. 'I'm glad it's not just my imagination. I do feel rough,' he admitted. 'This pain goes right through to my back—it's awful.'

'Don't worry, we'll sort you out,' she assured him with more confidence than she felt.

She paged Max, and told him, and he sounded less than thrilled.

'Better get him up to Theatre fast. Sounds like an aorta.'

'That's what I thought,' she said, beginning to panic. 'He's got bruising down the inside of his thighs, coming down the femoral canal. I must have missed it on Sunday.'

Max just grunted. 'I'll see you in Theatre in a minute,' he told her.

She found the ward sister, and within minutes Mr Andrews was up in Theatre and she was opening him up again, with Max standing over her like an avenging angel.

Please, God, she prayed, don't let me have made a mistake. Don't let him die.

'Get some retractors in there and get all that bowel out of the way,' Max snapped. 'Let's get a look at this fast.'

He didn't like the look of the patient's colour at all, and unless he'd missed his guess—

'His pressure's dropping,' Dick said crisply.

'I don't doubt it,' Max retorted, reaching in and shifting the bowel with his left hand, too impatient to wait for Annie.

She hooked the retractors round the bowel, held it out of the way and they peered in.

Mr Andrews's aorta had ruptured behind the peritoneum, the lining of the abdomen, and so the blood was trapped by the bulging membrane. Every heartbeat stretched it more, and it was going to go with a heck of a pop any second.

Repairing it was a highly skilled job, better suited to a vascular surgeon, but there wasn't a specialist in the hospital at the moment. Max could do it, but it was going to test Annie's skills to the limit.

'Right, this is what you have to do,' he told her, and explained, pointing to the area at the top and the bottom where she would have to make the connection with the supporting graft they used to repair the structure.

She nodded, asked a question, then squared her shoulders and began. He helped her, holding things with his left hand, pointing, directing, trying not to twitch when she was too slow, and then finally the aorta was repaired, and they released the clamp at the top to allow the blood to flow again.

Angie was bagging blood into the patient as fast as she could, and once the area was cleaned up and rinsed out, they could have a proper look at the damage and how it had arisen.

'How did I miss it?' Annie asked, sounding shocked. For a moment Max hesitated, then his natural honesty came to the fore. He couldn't leave her in doubt of her professional competence. She'd done an excellent job, both today and on Sunday.

'You may not have done,' he said. 'And anyway, when you opened him up you were looking at the spleen—and you've made a good job of it. The aorta may well have been silent—a tiny split in one layer of the wall, gradually deteriorating over time. There may have been nothing to see, like Tim Jacobs. Did I miss the tear in his mesenteric artery, or did it appear later? Who can tell?'

He shrugged. 'Surgery is a pretty inexact science. We do what we can, but sometimes things get missed, and the body tends to be quite forgiving and good at warning us.' He stared at the aortic graft, checking it for leaks, for kinks or bulges or problems of any sort, and then nodded with satisfaction.

'Whatever, it seems you've done it OK. He's safe now, barring clots getting to the wrong place. We'd better get him on some serious anticoagulant and then we can only hope he recovers well. He was lucky to get this far. Well done. You can close now.'

He turned away, stripping off his gloves with care, wincing as the tight latex pressed down on his fracture. He struggled with the ties of his gown, and finally got it off, then the hat and mask, and he poured himself a cup of coffee, stirred four sugars into it and sat down.

He was shaking all over, either from low blood sugar or pain or emotional turmoil—or all of the above, he admitted. He dropped his head back against the wall and let his breath out on a shaky sigh.

He was a father. Only—he checked the clock on the wall, and saw it was ten-thirty—seven and a half hours to go before he got to meet his daughter. He just had to get through the rest of the day…

Annie closed up Mr Andrews's incision, and stepped back with a shaky sigh. Hopefully everything would now be all right, and with any luck she wouldn't have to work alongside Max again for a day or two.

It had been agony, watching the impatience on his face, the suppressed irritation as he'd obviously wanted to take over. Well, that was his fault, because if he hadn't broken his hand he could have done the whole thing and Mike could have assisted him.

And she wouldn't have had to stand there opposite him with those frowning eyebrows so close to her, hideously conscious of her every move and the inadequacy of her performance.

She left the operating room, shouldering the door out of the way as she stripped off her gloves, and felt a pang of disappointment because Max was gone. Silly, really, because being with him was torture, but her stupid, foolish heart ached for his presence.

And tonight he was coming round to meet Alice, and it should have been such a wonderfully happy occasion, and instead it was going to be agony.

Oh, damn.

She squeezed her eyes shut, ripped off her mask and hat and gown and opened her eyes again to find Max standing there, dressed again in his normal clothes, his face a shuttered mask.

'Everything all right?' he asked gruffly.

'I take it you're talking about Mr Andrews?'

'I was.'

'He's fine.'

'Good.'

He left then, and she slumped into one of the chairs and sighed. Just seven hours to go, and he'd be meeting Alice.

* * *

Alice was beautiful. She had a huge smile, just like her mother's, but her eyes were his, so like his that he could have been looking into a mirror, and in her delicately pretty face the dark lashes made them seem even bigger and more striking.

She was tiny for her age, dainty and featherweight, and she settled on his lap with a gummy smile and pulled the pen out of his top pocket.

'You'd better take your jacket off before she makes a mess of it,' Annie warned, scooping the baby up. Max shrugged his jacket off and hung it over the back of the chair before taking his daughter back into his arms.

His daughter.

Amazing. He felt his eyes fill, and blinked hard. 'She's beautiful,' he said gruffly.

'Yes.'

He felt a sudden ache of loss for having missed her birth and those precious early weeks, and his anger began to rise in him again. He put it away with deliberate firmness. Now was not the time. The baby would pick up on it and that would be a shame.

He smiled at her, and she beamed back at him and grabbed his nose with her hand, hauling herself to her feet.

He winced and helped her up, supporting her as she jumped up and down on his lap giggling hugely and hanging onto his ears. Then she fell against him, her soft, wet rosebud mouth planting itself on his lips, and he kissed her and held her away, ignoring the pain in his hand.

'Hello, baby,' he said softly. 'I'm your daddy. What do you think of that?'

She blew a raspberry, and he chuckled quietly and hugged her, but she pushed away and started jumping again, each little leap grinding the bones in his hand together. Tough. It was his own fault he'd hurt it, and he wasn't going to stop her using him as a trampoline if that was what she wanted to do.

'I'll heat her supper,' Annie said, and went out into the kitchen, but Alice turned her head and watched her mother go, and started to wail.

'Come on, love, we'll go and watch, shall we? She's only next door.'

He followed Annie, to find her standing at the sink with her hands over her face, her shoulders heaving silently.

'Is there anything I can do?' he asked, feeling awkward and miserable and angry with both of them for the mess they were making of this whole thing.

'No. Just take her into the sitting room and entertain her. I won't be long.' Her voice was clogged with tears, and his heart ached for her, even though it was all her fault.

What a mess.

He took the unhappy baby back into the sitting room and tried to entertain her, but she was hungry and grizzly and she wanted her mother. All he could do was walk up and down with her in his arms, rocking her and crooning to her, and just hope that Annie would be quick.

She was, and he deliberately ignored her tear-stained face and focused instead on uniting Alice and her sloppy, messy food.

How hard could it be to get food into a baby? Everyone made it look so easy, but most of it seemed to be on her chin or her cheeks or down her bib—or all over him, come to that. She just shut her mouth at the wrong time, or turned her head, and his broken hand was awkward.

He tried with his left, but that was just worse, and in the end he gave up.

'Annie, I can't do this,' he admitted, and she took the baby from him without a word and spooned the food quickly and efficiently into her waiting mouth.

He couldn't bath her either, not with his hand in this state, but he'd brought a camera.

'Do you mind if I take photos of her?'

'So long as I'm not in the picture,' she said flatly.

So he took pictures, with Annie carefully off the edge of the field of view, and then after Alice was bathed and tucked up in bed, he kissed her goodnight, swallowing the lump in his throat, and then left the room.

He stood outside, listening to Annie singing to her, and then after a few minutes she came out, tears streaming down her face, and looked straight at him with red-rimmed eyes.

'You can go now,' she said, and he nodded, swallowed hard and headed for the door.

He got home just in time, fumbling his key in the lock and going in, closing the door behind him before the emotion of the past twenty-four hours caught up with him.

CHAPTER TEN

THE next few days were the longest of Annie's life, and even the nights couldn't bring oblivion. They were spent replaying their row, while she racked her brains for any other way she could have told Max about Alice, anything else she could have done that would have made it better, but there was nothing.

Apart from telling him straight away on his first day at the hospital, of course, and that was still impossible to contemplate and even more impossible to achieve now, after the event.

She was still deeply shocked at how fast he'd changed, one minute loving and affectionate, the next throwing her out of his house in a blazing temper. His words rang in her ears even now, days later, flaying her with every action replay.

'Get out. I don't want you here—not now, maybe not ever.'

And he'd made it clear every day since that he was only tolerating her presence to gain access to his daughter.

She, the faithless little minx, had taken to him like a duck to water after that first tense evening. He still couldn't bath her because of his broken hand, but he'd managed to feed her and dress her after her bath, although that was a bit hit and miss with her wriggling so much as he blew raspberries on her tummy.

Annie swallowed hard. They got on so well, and he was proving to be a wonderful and natural father. Just what she'd wanted, really, but impossibly difficult to reconcile with the man who looked straight through her and spoke only when absolutely necessary.

Annie went to work on Friday, dreading the day ahead, but in fact it wasn't too difficult. They didn't have a list, and Max kept firmly out of her way.

Mr Andrews had been moved from the geriatric ward, where he'd been at first, to ICU after his aortic graft, and was now back on the surgical ward where he belonged, together with his wife and son who had also been involved in the collision on Sunday.

His wife's parents, who had been travelling in the back of the people carrier, were on the orthopaedic ward, and Mr Andrews was the only one of the family in Max's care. His wife and son had been treated by David Armstrong and Nick Sarazin, and they were all progressing well. They were in the same bay together, and greeted Annie with affection when she walked in.

'It's my favourite doctor,' Mr Andrews said with a smile.

She ran a critical eye over him and smiled back. 'You look better today.'

'I feel better. I feel much better. I expect the physio will be round in a minute and ruin all that, but until then I'm just enjoying it.'

She laughed. 'You do that. I passed her in the corridor a minute ago, so she won't be long. I just want to have a look at your stomach.'

She pulled the screens round and examined him, and nodded her satisfaction. 'That looks and feels good. Your bowel sounds are returning, so you should be able to have something to eat later today. I want you to take it easy, though. Small drinks first, then graduate to semi-solids. You might get chicken soup tonight if you're really lucky!'

'I normally hate chicken soup, but I have to say I'm ready for it!' he said with a chuckle. 'Can I have a nice ham sandwich to wash it down?'

'Don't push your luck,' she warned, but she was smiling. She opened the curtains just as Max walked up, and she froze for a second.

'Morning,' he said vaguely to everyone. 'How are things?'

'Excellent, Mr Williamson, excellent,' Mr Andrews said, oblivious to the tension. 'I was just telling Annie I fancy a ham sandwich.'

'Maybe tomorrow,' she said encouragingly, and then braced herself for Max's criticism. It didn't come, though. Instead, he just nodded and walked away again, so with a mental shrug she carried on.

Mrs Bradley was ready to go home, and Annie was on her way to discharge her when she found Max there already.

'I think you could go home today,' he was saying, so with another shrug she turned away and went and made herself useful elsewhere. There was plenty to do, following up the other post-ops, discharging other patients that had come in for elective surgery and were ready to go home.

By the time she'd finished doing that Max had made himself scarce, and she was able to relax again.

Not for long, though, or at least not long enough.

He was round that evening as usual, playing with the baby, feeding her, making her giggle, and then while Annie was bathing her he said, 'I'd like my mother to see her.'

Annie felt sick. It was another step towards losing her daughter, another person to share her with, but Alice had a right to her grandparents as well as her father.

'When?' she asked, her voice taut.

'Tomorrow? She lives in Cambridge. I'll have to go and fetch her, she doesn't have a car.'

She shrugged. It didn't matter what she felt, it was going to happen anyway, and it would be too petty to refuse.

'Fine,' she agreed. 'What time?'

'I don't know. The morning, probably. Can I give you a ring?'

So formal! So horribly distant and remote. Oh, lord.

'Of course,' she said expressionlessly. 'Here, you can dry her.'

She scooped the baby out of the bath, let her drip for a second then plonked her on the towel on his lap and left them to it. Anything to get away from him and that icy politeness.

'I've got something to tell you.'

'Really? Sounds exciting. Sit yourself down, you're cluttering up my kitchen.' Max's mother put the kettle on, swiped a damp cloth over the worktop and then turned to him, cloth in hand. 'Well? What is it?'

Where to start? Nowhere, he realised, that would avoid the lecture that was inevitably coming.

'I've got a baby,' he said, and his mother sat down on the other chair with a plonk and stared at him.

'Nothing like getting straight to the point,' she said. 'Would you care to elaborate?'

He sighed and rammed a hand through his hair. 'I suppose so. Her name's Alice, and she's eight months old.'

'Eight months? Good grief,' she said faintly. 'Have you only just found out?'

He nodded. 'Yes—on Monday night.'

There was a long pause. 'And how did you find out?' his mother prodded gently.

'Annie told me.'

'Annie?'

He sighed heavily, and his mother sat back and looked at him over the table, a patient look on her face.

'Why don't you start at the beginning?' she suggested, so he did, telling her all about how he'd met her, how they'd just gelled, how wonderful it had been to be with her.

'It just…happened. I can't explain or excuse it. She was married, I was engaged. It was way out of order, but— It was just so right somehow, more right than anything's ever felt before.'

'And then you lost touch, presumably?'

He nodded. 'We agreed we couldn't see each other again, because she had a husband and I was marrying Fiona—except, of course, I couldn't, not after that. I know it sounds really crass, but I felt as if I'd touched heaven with Annie, and my relationship with Fiona was such a pale imitation in comparison. And anyway, she'd met her barrister by then.'

Max shrugged. 'So that was it. I thought I'd never see Annie again, and then when I started working at the Audley, there she was suddenly, as large as life and my junior registrar. I couldn't believe it, and I felt just the same about her as I had a year ago. I was just stunned, and then after a week she told me Alice was mine.'

He felt a wave of nausea just remembering that awful night, all the soul-baring that had gone on before she'd told him, and how raw and exposed and cheated he'd felt afterwards.

'And her husband? Where does he figure in all this?'

Max blinked and looked back at his mother. 'Sorry, didn't I mention it? Her husband's dead. He died of cancer last year.'

His mother's face registered shock and then compassion. 'Good heavens. Poor girl. How awful for her. And then she had a baby in the midst of all of that. Oh, poor child.' She shook her head slowly in disbelief. 'So, if it's not a stupid question, how does she know Alice is yours?'

'The eyes,' he said flatly. 'It's like looking in a mirror.'

Her mother gave a sad smile. 'Your father always said that after you were born,' she said softly, and her eyes misted over, remembering him. 'So,' she went on, pulling herself together visibly, 'what happens now?'

He gave a huff of humourless laughter. 'Now—

well, now I'm trying to get to know my daughter without killing Annie for having kept it from me.'

'But she couldn't have told you,' his mother said matter-of-factly. 'Did she know where you were? And anyway, you'd agreed not to see each other again, and she thought you were married, didn't she?'

He nodded. 'Yes, but…when we met again, she could have told me then, for heaven's sake, but she just kept it a secret and said nothing for a week! She even had the gall to tell me she wanted to be sure of me!'

His mother stared at him blankly. 'What's wrong with that?' she asked, sounding genuinely puzzled.

'What's wrong with it? Mother, she was testing me! I was being vetted, for God's sake!'

'So?' His mother stood up and took two mugs down from the hooks under the cupboard and spooned coffee into them, totally unconcerned, or so it seemed. She poured the water onto the granules, stirred each cup twice, tapped the spoon on the side of the mugs—he was ready to strangle her by the time she sat down.

'Is this anything to do with your broken hand?' she asked, and he growled under his breath.

'I hit the wall,' he admitted, and his mother tutted at him.

'You always did have a shocking temper. You'd think by the age of thirty-two you would have got a grip on it. So why were you so mad with her?' she went on calmly.

He counted to ten and breathed in and out deeply before replying. 'She didn't trust me,' he said, slowly and carefully, as if his mother were a little dense. 'She was checking me out to make sure I wasn't just a promiscuous philanderer, unquote.'

'Very sensible girl. She didn't know you from Adam.'

'I'm your son!' he yelled, outraged, and she quelled him with a single look.

'You're being ridiculous,' she told him crisply. 'I know you, of course I do, but she doesn't, and this is her baby we're talking about, don't forget. You'd make that much fuss about lending someone your car!'

'She's my baby, too,' he growled, but she shook her head.

'Oh, no, she isn't. You might have been there at her conception, but that doesn't make her your baby. Who gave birth to her? Who carried her for nine months? Who walks up and down the floor all night with her when she can't sleep, and plays with her when she's happy, and feeds her and cares for her? No, Max, I'm sorry, she's Annie's baby, and she was absolutely right to vet you before telling you, or at least to give herself time to decide how she wanted to play your relationship.'

'Oh, she did that, all right,' he said bitterly. 'She waited until I asked her to marry me.'

'So she could be sure you loved her for herself and weren't just doing the decent thing? Tell me, Max. Was she happy with her first husband?'

He shook his head. 'No.'

'So she wouldn't have wanted to make another mistake.'

He sighed harshly and shook his head again. Since when had his mother been so damned logical? 'No.'

'Well, then, I rest my case. Drink your coffee and take me to see this baby. I'd like to meet my first grandchild, and my future daughter-in-law.'

'I shouldn't hold your breath on that one,' he advised her bitterly. 'There won't be any wedding.'

'But…you said you'd asked her to marry you.'

'Before she told me.'

'Oh, what, and now she's been sensible and a caring mother and not put herself first, you've had a fit of masculine pride and dumped her? Max! How old are you? For heaven's sake, grow up!'

She snatched the coffee out of his hand and poured it down the sink. 'We're going now—and while I get to know Alice, you and Annie are going to have a serious heart-to-heart.'

'Mother, butt out—'

'No. You're a fool, Max, a bigger fool than even I would have given you credit for. Just answer me one thing. Do you love her?'

His heart felt as if a giant hand had crushed it. 'Oh, yes, I love her,' he said softly. 'She's my other half.'

'Then you need to tell her that, and stop flouncing around in a fit of pique before you've thrown it all away.'

Was that all it was? A fit of pique? Max was silent and thoughtful all the way back to Audley, and when they pulled up outside Annie's house his heart was pounding.

His mother was right. He'd been an idiot, and he'd probably ruined his only real chance of happiness in this lifetime. Please, God, don't let it be too late, he said silently as he helped his mother from the car and rang the doorbell.

They were expected—he'd phoned on his mobile and warned Annie when he would be there—and she came to the door with Alice propped on her hip, a cautious smile on that beautiful and generous mouth that he loved so much.

'Mum, this is Annie,' he said. 'Annie, my mother, Margaret. And this is Alice.'

His mother's eyes flooded with tears and she put her arms around both of them and hugged them gently. 'Oh, my dear girl, what a beautiful little baby,' she said unsteadily. 'Hello, Alice. I'm your grandma.'

'Would you like to hold her?' Annie asked, but Margaret shook her head.

'No. Well, I would, but…give her time. She doesn't know who I am, and she's not a toy. You're lovely, aren't you, sweetheart?'

And Alice, as if sensing the love emanating from her grandmother, launched herself at her with a gurgle of laughter.

'I think that's all the time she needs,' Annie said, and relinquished her hold on her daughter with a little flicker of pain that she couldn't quite hide.

Oh, Annie, how could I have got it so wrong? Max thought, his heart aching. You did it for Alice, all of it. Oh, lord. What a fool I've been.

'Come on in,' Annie was saying, ushering them into the hall. And then her parents were there to meet his mother, his father giving Max stony looks over everyone's heads.

'Come into the drawing room, I've made coffee,'

Jill was saying, and they trailed after her, all of them equally uncomfortable and awkward. Max sat on the window-seat out of the way, and watched as his mother charmingly and expertly engineered the conversation onto neutral territory while Alice bounced happily on her lap.

Then she sat down suddenly and started to chew her fist and grizzle, and Annie took her back.

'Time for her lunch,' she said with a fleeting smile that didn't reach her eyes, and headed for the door.

Max got to his feet and followed her. His mother was well able to take care of herself, and he needed to talk to Annie.

'Excuse me, time for my next lesson,' he said with an equally fleeting smile, and grabbed the door just before Annie shut it in his face.

'I can manage,' she told him crisply, but he shook his head.

'I know you can. That's not what this is about.'

'What is it about? You want another fight? Want to pick holes in how I'm looking after her—or have you decided to tell me you're going for custody?'

He felt sick. He'd been through all of those things in his head, and rejected them. Now all he wanted to do was take her in his arms.

'I want to talk to you,' he said.

'So talk. You have a captive audience. I can't promise to listen, though.'

His heart sank. She wasn't going to make it easy for him, obviously, but, then, he probably didn't deserve that. He was finding it hard to think of anything she could give him that he'd deserve, apart from permanent marching orders, and that was probably about to come any second.

Annie was truly angry, hurt and disillusioned and not in the least inclined to cut Max any slack, but then she looked up at him and saw the misery on his face and the pain in those wonderful ice-blue eyes, and she relented.

'So, what did you want to say?' she asked with a weary sigh.

He shook his head. 'Not here. Can you feed Alice and leave her with all the grandparents? Please?'

It was the 'please' that did it. That and the look in his eyes, as if he'd been to hell and back.

She understood that. She'd spent the whole of the last week on that journey, except she'd had a one-way ticket.

'OK. I'll see if they mind.'

'I'll feed her if you like,' he offered, and she handed the grizzly baby to him while she heated the food and tested it on the inside of her wrist.

'OK, OK, it's coming,' she told Alice, and clipped her plastic bib on.

Max sat down and got the first spoonful in, and after that all was peace. Tense, strained, but relatively quiet at least.

Then finally Alice was finished, her nappy was changed and Annie took her through to the drawing room.

'Mum, would you mind watching her for me for a while? Max wants to talk.'

'Can't you do that here?' her father said, bristling a little, but she shook her head.

'No. I'm sorry. I don't know how long we'll be. She'll need a sleep soon, so she won't be much trouble.'

'Don't worry, darling, we'll be fine,' her mother said firmly, quelling her father with a look. 'You go.'

Max's mother gave Annie a reassuring smile, and she squared her shoulders and went back out to the hall. Max was standing by the front door, and she couldn't read the expression on his face because of the light behind him.

'OK?' he asked, and she nodded.

He opened the door, ushered her into the car and drove round to his house in silence. She could feel the tension coming off him in waves, and her heart was pounding so loudly she couldn't hear herself think.

He walked her to the door, opened it and ushered her inside, then the door closed with a decisive click.

'Do you want a drink?' he offered, but she shook her head. She thought if she ate or drank anything, she'd be sick. She hugged her arms around her waist to hold herself together.

'No. Just…say what you want to say, please, and get it over.'

Oh, lord, don't let it be custody, she begged silently. Not that. Anything but that.

He sighed, a shaky, ragged sigh that seemed ripped out of him, and then he lifted his head and met her eyes.

'I don't know where to start, except to say I'm sorry,' he said gruffly. 'I've been a fool—a proud, stupid fool. I got you all mixed up with Fiona, and decided you were just holding out for a consultant husband, and I was so incensed about you vetting me I just lost touch with what we were talking about.

'I completely forgot how you must feel, how protective of Alice. I just assumed you'd realise I'd feel the same about her, but why should you? As you pointed out, you didn't know me from Adam. Why should you trust me?'

Annie felt her eyes fill at his confession. 'I should have trusted myself,' she told him honestly. 'I knew you were all right. I'd been thinking for days that I must tell you, but I didn't know how. I wasn't sure how you'd react, but I knew by then that you had a great sense of honour and you'd do the decent thing, but I didn't *want* you to do the decent thing. I wanted you to want me for myself, so I kept Alice from you, and I shouldn't have done. I'm sorry.'

'*You're* sorry?' Max said, sounding stunned. 'Annie, you have nothing to be sorry for. I was just an idiot—just a mass of outraged pride and blind stupidity, and now you hate me.'

'I don't hate you!' she exclaimed. 'I love you—I'll always love you. I was just so hurt when you threw me out—'

'Oh, Annie.'

Suddenly his arms were round her, holding her hard against his chest, and she could hear his heart pounding beneath her ear.

'Tell me it's not too late,' he begged. 'Tell me I haven't lost you.'

'You haven't lost me,' she said tearfully. 'No way.

You can't lose me, Max. I won't be lost—not that easily.'

His arms tightened convulsively and he pressed his lips hard against her hair. 'Oh, my love,' he whispered tenderly. 'I thought—'

He broke off, lifting his head and threading his hands through her hair, staring down at her with his heart written in his eyes. 'I love you,' he said quietly. 'I'll always love you. My mother asked how I felt about you, and I told her you were my other half. It's true. I don't feel complete without you. I haven't, since the day I met you, and maybe even before that. There's always been something missing.'

'Until now.'

'Until now,' he echoed, and then he lowered his head and kissed her with tender reverence.

'Make love to me, Max,' she whispered. 'I've missed you.'

With a ragged groan he lifted his head and stared down into her eyes. 'I've missed you, too. I thought I'd lost you. I can't believe you're here with me.' He gave his hand a rueful grimace. 'Think you can manage to walk upstairs? I can't carry you, my hand isn't up to it.'

'It'd better mend soon,' she told him, her heart filled with happiness again. 'I'll expect you to carry me over the threshold when we're married, and I don't intend to wait for long.'

As she said it, she had an agonising second of doubt. They were still getting married, weren't they? But he hadn't said—

'I'll make an exception on our wedding day,' he

said with a slow smile, and she relaxed again. 'After all, considering how nearly it didn't happen, I reckon it'll be worth the sacrifice.'

'You're such a hero,' she teased. 'A bit dense on occasions, though. I can see I'm going to have to be careful to make sure you've understood—'

'Get upstairs, woman,' he said, pretending to scowl at her. 'You've got such a sassy mouth on you. I shall have to find a way of silencing you.'

'I can think of a good one,' she said, and, reaching up, she pulled his head down and kissed him.

'About the wedding.'

'Mmm?' she mumbled sleepily. Her head was pillowed on Max's chest, her legs entwined with his, and she was almost asleep for the first time in six days.

'You said you didn't want to wait long. Does that mean you don't want a big church wedding?'

Annie lifted her head, propped herself up on her elbows and looked down into his eyes. They were clear of pain now, his expression tender and caring. Much better.

'I don't care, so long as it's quick and we get married. I just want to be with you.'

'And your job? Do you want to carry on working, or do you want to stay at home and look after Alice?'

She sighed and dropped her head onto his chest again. 'I don't know. Mum seems quite happy to have her, but it seems a bit much to make it a long-term thing. I only agreed because I was in such a state and she'd been so closely involved with Alice since her birth.'

'I still haven't seen the photos.'

'No. You must. I expect my parents are showing your mother at the moment—unless they're lined up on opposite sides of the drawing room, daggers drawn.'

His chest rumbled with laughter. 'I hardly think so. My mother's made of sterner stuff than that. I expect they're trading life stories.'

His hand smoothed over her back, his fingers trailing down her spine. 'So, back to the wedding—do you want to get married in church or a register office?'

'I don't know. Church would be nice—or the hospital chapel. That's small and quite pretty. What about you?'

She felt him shrug. 'I don't know. I don't have any particular religious beliefs. I don't know about you, but I think the fact that we're together after all we've been through is nothing short of a miracle, really, and maybe I just want it sanctified. Does that sound silly?'

It didn't. It sounded like an echo of her own thoughts, and she told him so.

'Well, we can sort it out.' He shifted slightly so he could see her face and gave her a rueful smile. 'I hate to break this up when you're so comfortable, but do you think we should go and put our respective parents out of their misery?'

Annie sighed and snuggled closer. 'Five more minutes,' she murmured, and went straight to sleep.

'Annie? Annie, wake up, we're here.'

She opened her eyes and looked around her. Trees, tall trees, and a white house, and between the two, in the distance across the sweeping lawn, the dark blue water of Thirlmere.

Max was smiling at her, his eyes searching her face. 'OK?'

'Mmm. You?'

'Glad to be here. It's a long way.'

'But worth it?'

He smiled again. 'Oh, yes. Come on, let's go in. It'll be time for dinner soon.'

Her stomach rumbled, and he laughed. 'Come on, piglet. Let's be having you. I'll get the luggage in a minute.'

They went inside, and Hans greeted them with his usual cheer. 'Welcome, welcome,' he said, and moments later he'd shown them to their room.

'It's got a four-poster,' she said, laughing with delight. 'And a lake view.'

'Nothing but the best for my wife,' Max said, coming up behind her as she stood at the window and slipping his arms around her waist. His head rested against hers, and for a moment he was silent.

Then he said, very gently, 'Are you all right about this? I mean, with Peter and everything?'

She nodded. 'Yes. I've put Peter to rest. All my memories of this place are of you, but there is one thing I have to do.'

She turned to him and gave him a quiet smile. 'Can you give me a minute alone? I just want to go outside.'

'Of course.'

She squeezed his hand, then went out of the hotel and down to the water. She had a flower in her hand, a carnation that she'd pulled out of the arrangement in the entrance hall, and she stood at the water's edge in silence for a moment, thinking of Peter.

He was a distant memory now, but she owed him this.

'I'm sorry,' she said softly. 'Sorry for all of it. But I'm happy now, and I wanted to thank you for bringing me here so that I met Max. Goodbye, Peter.'

She threw the carnation out onto the water, and watched it float there for a moment. Then a little flurry of wind came out of nowhere and carried it out of sight, and she felt peace steal over her.

With a smile on her lips, she turned and walked back up the path to Max and the rest of her life…

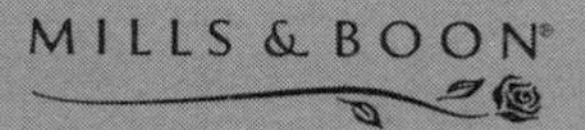

Medical Romance™

A DOCTOR'S HONOUR ***by Jessica Matthews***

Gavin and Aly seemed destined to marry – until Gavin lost the battle to save Aly's cousin. He blamed himself, and felt compelled to leave town and the woman he loved. Three years later Aly found a way for Gavin to return. Her clinic desperately needed a doctor – and she desperately needed to convince Gavin they still had a future!

A FAMILY OF THEIR OWN ***by Jennifer Taylor***

Nurse Leanne Russell left Australia in search of her real mother – she found Dr Nick Slater. She's dreamed of a family of her own and now she knows she wants that family with Nick. But Nick has vowed never to marry – it wouldn't be fair to have children. Unless his love for Leanne is enough to persuade him to take a chance...

PARAMEDIC PARTNERS ***by Abigail Gordon***

Trainee paramedic Selina Sanderson feels the electricity as soon as she sets eyes on her gorgeous new boss. She soon realises her feelings are deep – but why is he so uncomfortable with a female partner? Kane wants more than anything to be part of Selina's life – but if she discovers the secret he's trying to leave behind she might never trust him again...

On sale 6th September 2002

Available at most branches of WH Smith, Tesco, Martins, Borders, Eason, Sainsbury's and most good paperback bookshops.

0802/03a